THE LONG DROP

"Longarm, why would any man want to tell an ugly cuss like you where he hid the take from that last bank job?"

Longarm shrugged and suggested, "You ain't about to come back for it. You might rate your name in the papers some more, and that gal you left back home might read your name if the money was recovered instead of just rotting away where you buried it."

They were out in the yard, now. The thirteen steps and the platform they led up to still stood in purple shade. They had him at the foot of those steps to eternity now, but Prentiss dug in his heel and said, "Hold on, boys. I got things to talk over with my old checkers opponent, first."

The hangman gently but firmly suggested it was best to get on with it and get it over.

Longarm shook his head and said, "Let the man have his say."

Abner Prentiss suggested, "Why don't we have a set-down coffee whilst we talk this over, old son? The money will still be where I put it and my neck will be just as easy to bust at, hell, high noon if we have time to discuss the matter in-depth."

The hangman shook his head and said, "I got a job to do and he's just stalling for time."

Longarm nodded and the assistant hangmen on either side commenced to boost Prentiss up those thirteen steps whether his feet were touching any of them or not.

TABOR EVANS

LONGARM

AND THE DEAD MAN'S TALE

JOVE BOOKS, NEW YORK

LONGARM AND THE DEAD MAN'S TALE

A Jove Book / published by arrangement with
the author

PRINTING HISTORY
Jove edition / November 2003

ISBN: 0-515-13633-6

A JOVE BOOK®
Jove Books are published by The Berkley Publishing Group,
a division of Penguin Group (USA) Inc.,
375 Hudson Street, New York, New York 10014.
JOVE and the "J" design
are trademarks belonging to Penguin Group (USA) Inc.

PRINTED IN THE UNITED STATES OF AMERICA

10 9 8 7 6 5 4 3 2 1

Chapter 1

Death watch was a dismal detail but somebody had to pull it, and when it came your turn your only consolation was that the poor cuss they were fixing to hang in the morning was enjoying his last night a whole lot less than you were.

So Deputy U.S. Marshal Custis Long of the Denver District Court had shown up with plenty of three-for-a-nickel cheroots, a checker board, and some copies of *Captain Billy's Whizz Bang* to spend a last night in a patent cell with the soon-to-be-late Abner Prentiss and make sure he didn't kill himself before it was time for him to die.

They called the bolted-together boilerplate and bar-grill box from back East a patent cell because the steel mill that shipped them far and wide had patented that particular design. Other cell designs were shipped by other outfits under their own patents.

All of them were a bitch to escape from, once installed in a frame, 'dobe, or in this case stone-walled federal house of detention. Hence Longarm, as he was better known around the same, wasn't worried about the somewhat younger and way smaller condemned man escaping through the gray-green solid steel all around them as they played checkers in the wee small hours. He found it more distracting to have the washed-out-looking cuss asking him what time it was every other checker move.

Prentiss jumped two of Longarm's blacks with his red to weakly crow, "Hot damn! You never saw that coming, did you?"

"You're too slick for me by half," Longarm conceded.

So then, as tedious as the turgid waves of some dark sea of sewage sludge in caverns measureless to man, the poor simp asked, "What time you got, now, pard?"

Longarm said, "Four-fifteen. Give or take five."

"You never took out your watch," the prisoner pouted.

In a firm if not unkind tone Longarm replied, "Don't have to. You asked the same question less than five minutes ago. Ready for another smoke, kid?"

Prentiss smiled weakly and said, "Been trying to cut down for my health. Funny how tobacco tastes like smouldering rags, not a one of the jokes in them joke books seems funny, and winning four games in a row with you feels like I've been trying to jack off my big toe. You'd think an old boy about to say adios to life would enjoy life's little pleasures more, wouldn't you?"

Longarm didn't answer as he stared down at the checker board on the bunk between them, as if the game they were playing meant toad squat to either of them.

Prentiss said, "You've been letting me win, ain't you? Nobody plays that dumb by accident."

Longarm shrugged and said, "Checkers ain't my game. You were the one who said he didn't know how to play chess. I offered to *teach* you."

The pale blond Prentiss laughed weakly and asked, "Why the hell would any fool want to learn anything new the night before they were fixing to take him out and hang him?"

Longarm shrugged, and before he'd thought he'd said, "Seems to me you might have lived longer if you'd been

2

willing to learn new ways a good ways back along the Owlhoot Trail." Then he quickly added, "I'm sorry I said that, kid. Nobody appointed this child to be your judge and what's done is done."

Prentiss grimaced and said, "Four counts of murder in the first, even though I still say that one federal deputy drew first. But I follow your drift. We might not be holding this conversation out here in Colorado had I never left the old homestead back in Bleeding, Kansas."

He picked up a red checker, stared at it as if it were dog shit, and let it fall to the painted steel floor as he added, "Fuck it. I don't want to play no more. I *did* leave the old homestead back in Bleeding, Kansas, to ride with Bloody Bill Anderson against the Damn Yankees and I got so good at such riding I never stopped and now they're fixing to bust my neck and make me shit my pants and . . . Is it true I'll have a hard-on when they cut me down, Longarm?"

"Can't say," Longarm lied. "I ain't one for hanging around that long after . . . pulling this detail."

Prentiss sighed and said, "They tell me I'll have a swell hard-on once they've busted my neck like so. Seems like such a waste as soon as you consider a dead man's chances with the gals. What time is it?"

Longarm said, "Four-twenty, more or less. Weren't you a tad young to ride off to war with a guerrilla, kid? No offense, but you're younger than me and I barely squeezed in as the kid of my old outfit."

Abner Prentiss said, "I was twelve. Somebody from our family was expected to join up and my elder brothers were big sissies. They both lit out for Californee to prospect for gold when the call went out for volunteers along our wagon trace. My momma cried and carried on. But my pappy gifted me with the Hall rifle he'd carried down Mexico way and shook my hand, like I was a grown man, the day I left for the war. They'd told me I was signing

3

up as a drummer boy. But they didn't have no drums and I got me a fucking Free Stater with my pappy's Hall rifle the first raid I rode. Blew half that fucker's head off at nigh three hundred yards and after that they called me Eagle Chick. What time is it?"

Longarm said, "You just asked. Can't be four-thirty yet. Lots of old boys blew fuckers' heads off in the war, kid. Most of us cut down on the habit after Appomattox."

Prentiss shrugged and said, "Tried to go back to farming after I got home, dressed to the nines in an officer's uniform with my share of a bank robbery we staged as a sort of defeat celibation. Steering a plow ahint a mule as old as I was somehow failed to cut the mustard for me. I *tried*, mind you, but the second or third day, as that fool mule lifted its tail to shit in my face some more, I just left it hitched to the plow out in our west forty and never tried to explain my leaving. What time is it?"

"A little after four-thirty. Sure you ain't ready for a smoke?" the older lawman quietly replied.

The condemned man said, "I reckon. Is it true they give you a day off after . . . a night like this? What time is it?"

Longarm handed Prentiss a cheroot as he said, "Four-thirty-five or so. They don't expect me to show up at the federal building up near Capitol Hill this morning. It will have been a long sleepless night, and fair is fair."

Prentiss laughed harshly and said, "Long for you, not for me, and you're so right about sleepless. Have you ever sat up like this with a man who *slept* his last night away?"

Longarm said, "Matter of fact, I have. It don't happen all that often but some old boys seem creatures of habit, or possessed of a tad less imagination than the rest of us."

Prentiss counted in his head and decided, "I got less'n an hour and a half to stay awake and then I get to sleep forever, I hope. What do you reckon happens after we die, Longarm?"

The tall dark lawman soberly replied, "Don't know.

4

Farther along, as the old church song has it, we'll know all about it. All of us. From my limited experience on this side, the stars don't go out when we die and the sun also rises as the world goes on without us. But if it's any comfort the world we leave is a different world than it would have been if we'd never passed through it."

Prentiss asked, "What time is it? What do you mean? How can you say this world is going to know I was ever here, once I'm gone?"

Longarm said, "Going on twenty to five, I reckon. We, all of us, change the world around us with every breath we take, whether that much change in the atmosphere shows or not. We, all of us, leave bigger tracks, good and bad, from cradle to grave, because we just can't help it. As we brush by others we make 'em laugh, we make 'em cuss, or sometimes we make 'em weep. Every fool kid who ever carved his initials in a tree trunk left his world a different place than it might have been. Had you and that mule finished plowing that field that day this world would be different, whether you robbed that bank a week later or not."

Prentiss stared off through solid steel to muse, "Forty acres of flint corn more or less must have changed things some for somebody. I planted some apple trees one time. Do you reckon that made this world just a little bit nicer than if I hadn't?"

Longarm nodded as he began to put the checkers and their board away. Picking that one off the floor gave a man something to *do* as a steel door clanged in the near distance and footsteps ran along the cement flooring of the corridor outside.

Abner Prentiss stared goggle-eyed at Longarm to gasp, "You've been lying about the time all this time! Why didn't you tell me what time it really was when I asked you what time it was, Longarm?"

Longarm didn't answer. The execution party paused

outside the bars and the warden gravely said, "Pursuant to the wishes of this condemned prisoner, no chaplain has been assigned to this detail. It is not, however, too late to request religious consultation should the prisoner so desire."

Abner Prentiss rose to his full but less than imposing height with a game or defiant smile to say, "Told your sky pilot not to pester me with prayers for mercy and forgivings. Told him you ain't about to show no mercy and I never would have done half the things I done if I thought anyone on high was *watching*!"

The cell door opened. The hangman's assistants entered to take hold of Prentiss and steer him out to the yard where the gallows waited by the dawn's early light.

Prentiss asked, "You coming, Longarm?"

Rising higher than anyone else in the cell, with the checker set under his arm but the humor magazines left for the next occupant, the weary Longarm replied, "Up to you, kid."

Prentiss said, "I got things to tell you. Things you've brung back from long ago and far away and . . . Shit, I meant what I said about sky pilots."

So Longarm fell in beside the condemned man as the dead march set out down the corridor. Longarm was too polite, and too good at questioning suspects, to break out his notebook as Prentiss grumbled, "I doubt any mealy-mouthed preacher would understand, but I do feel sort of glad about one fork in the trail I took, starting out along said trail. There was this gal, back home, a home gal who said she'd be my woman along the Owlhoot Trail if only I'd let her ride it with me. She said she'd cook and sew or tend my wounds with kisses if only I would carry her along with me. But, like I said, she was a home gal, barely sixteen, soaking wet, and I didn't have it in me to take her with me. Ain't that a bitch?"

"You did the right thing," Longarm soberly replied.

Prentiss sighed and said, "I reckon. But she was so damned pretty and I wanted her so bad I could taste it and I can't count the nights I kicked myself for being so noble when I could have had me all that swell fucking."

Longarm didn't answer. Nobody else in the execution detail could come up with an intelligent comment, either.

So in the end Abner Prentiss decided, "This morning I see for certain I made the right choice. This old world I'm leaving *is* a better place than it might have been because, the last I heard, that only gal I ever loved wound up with a good man who's provided well for her and their four kids better than any fool outlaw could have, robbing *twice* as many banks!"

Longarm quietly suggested, "I'm sure you're right about your sweetheart being better off with another. But ain't you being a tad modest about your accomplishments, kid? They caught you less 'n a week after that last big score and you only had fifty-eight dollars on you after riding off with close to fifty thousand. Are you the one and original big spender or is it safe to assume you cached a whole lot of money somewhere along that Owlhoot Trail?"

They were out in the yard now. The crisp morning air smelled like burning autumn leaves. It wasn't autumn. It didn't matter. It always smelled like someone was burning autumn leaves in downtown Denver. The sky above was a cloudless bowl of cobalt blue. Sharply slanting sunlight shone off the gallows' beam high above. The thirteen steps and the platform they led up to still stood in purple shade. The man about to mount those thirteen steps said, "Nice try, Longarm. But why would any man who told the sky pilots to go fuck themselves want to tell an ugly cuss like you where he hid the take from that last bank job?"

Longarm shrugged and suggested, "You ain't about to come back for it. You might rate your name in the papers somemore, and that gal you left back home might read your name if the money was recovered instead of just rotting away where you buried it."

They had him at the foot of the steps to eternity now, but Prentiss dug in his heel and said, "Hold on, boys. I got things to talk over with my old checkers opponent first."

The hangman gently but firmly suggested it was best to get on with it and get it over.

Longarm shook his head and said, "Let the man have his say."

So they did, and Abner Prentiss said, "It ain't rotting in the ground. I prized up the floorboards of this one place I stayed, and put the money bags betwixt the joists above the fucking wine theater downstairs."

"Where did all this happen? In what town?" Longarm asked.

Abner Prentiss suggested, "Why don't we go have a set-down coffee whilst we talk it over, old son? The money will still be where I put it and my neck will be just as easy to bust at, hell, high noon if we have time to discuss the matter in-depth."

The hangman shook his head at Longarm and said, "I got a job to do and he's just stalling for time."

Longarm nodded and the assistant hangmen on either side commenced to boost Prentiss up those thirteen steps whether his feet were touching any of them or not.

He was wailing something about wanting to talk to that sky pilot after all as Longarm turned away to cross the yard and get out of it whilst the getting was good. For when you'd watched one hanging you'd seen enough and now, goddamn it, he couldn't take the morning off before he'd reported in to tell his boss, Marshal Billy Vail, what he'd just figured out about all those missing federal funds.

Chapter 2

The gilt letters on the oaken door read U.S. MARSHAL WIL-LIAM VAIL, but when you went inside the first thing you saw was a long, pale drink of water playing the typewriter. Old Henry looked up from his typing to ask, "What are you doing here so early on a work day? Didn't you pull death watch last night?"

Longarm handed him the checker set, saying, "Shove this up your ass, or find another place to file it, Henry. Boss in the back?"

Henry demurely asked, "Did the sun come up this morning? It's going on seven A.M. but you're not sup-posed to be here."

Longarm muttered, "I know," as he strode back to the inner sanctum of their mutual superior, lighting a cheroot along the way in self-defense.

He knocked once lest he catch anybody jerking off and went on in to find Vail's ever-stuffy oak-paneled office already reeking of expensive but awesomely pungent ci-gar smoke. The older, shorter, stubbier lawman behind the cluttered desk didn't look surprised to see his senior dep-uty at that hour. Billy Vail had risen through the ranks by being smart. He said, "Morning, old son. Where did Abner Prentiss say he'd hidden all that money?"

Longarm took a seat across from his boss without waiting to be invited, flicked ash on the rug, and said, "They strung him up just as we were getting around to that. But he did let slip some shit about a hired room above a wine theater and they picked him up in Leadville a few days after he hit that unfortunately located private bank on the military reserve at Camp Weld."

Billy Vail chortled, "Never ride off with funds marked as federal- and state-guard payrolls even when you think you're too slick for your poor old Uncle Sam."

Taking a puff that would have done an Indian smoke signal proud, and then erupting like a self-satisfied volcano, Vail pontificated, "He thought we'd think robbers hitting a bank just south of Denver would make for Denver's handy Union Depot, with a view to leaving for other parts by rail, when he actually rode alone over the Front Range with his share of the ill-gotten gains. What do you reckon his share would've been, old son?"

"All of it," Longarm replied, observing, "Three masked riders hit that bitty branch bank at Camp Weld. Two bloated bodies, later identified as known bank robbers, were fished out of the South Platte a short time after their old pal Abner was arrested in that Leadville house of ill repute. Do we really need chalk marks on a blackboard in here?"

Vail smiled thinly and said, "Not hardly. He always was a sweet kid and leopards wouldn't have changed their spots since he pulled the same stunt on those pickup riders in Nebraska last year. So we're talking close to fifty, in a wine theater, you say?"

Longarm said, "There's a lot of that going around up in Leadville since the real Grand Central Theatre opened up yonder, to be replaced by the Tabor Opera House, the Comiquque, Gaiety, and New Theatres that staged such shows as *Around the World in 80 Days*. So bigger saloons installed orchestra pits and raised stages along back walls as they applied for special licenses as so-called wine theaters, where you get to hit the suckers with a cover charge as long as you put on a show for 'em every now and again."

He let that sink in and added, "They didn't offer a stage show at the whorehouse where the Leadville law arrested Prentiss for us. We can eliminate all the wine theaters that don't hire rooms out for . . . Hold the thought. He never said it was a room he was *staying* in."

Billy Vail nodded approvingly and volunteered, "Rooms with beds up above a wine theater usually come equipped with bed mates. How do you feel about a less-often-visited costume or storage loft above all the fun and games?"

Longarm flicked more ash and decided. "Adds up better. As old a hand at the game as young Prentiss was, he'd have expected us to search his last-known address if we cut his trail. Nobody found shit in the whorehouse he'd been staying at and had he beat the rap . . . That works pretty good. Your call, boss."

Vail blew an octopus cloud of pungent smoke and studied it a time before he decided. "The local law could shake down every wine theater for us in less time than it would take you to get up to Leadville. So what's wrong with that easy solution—and watch those fucking ashes on my fucking rug! Ain't you got no manners at all?"

Longarm easily replied, "I might, if you ever saw fit to let Henry put a fucking ashtray out for this side of your fucking desk. As to telling the other kids that a cuss we just hung might or might not have hidden fifty thousand easter eggs for them to look for without adult supervision . . . I got to catch at least a few hours of sleep before I head on up yonder, though."

Vail said, "If you catch the next train and catch a few daylight winks at your hotel up yonder . . . Forget I just

11

said anything that dumb and watch those fucking *ashes*, damn your eyes!"

Longarm said, "Tobacco ash is good for carpet mites. I read that in a book one time. I'm glad we agree any wise-money boys up Leadville way could wind up wondering what I was doing in town long before I got to do shit in their town if I lay slugabed in a Leadville hotel."

Vail snorted. "Did that book say whether tobacco ash was good for carpet mites because it killed 'em or *fed* 'em? Get on home and sleep some cobwebs away, as long as you make it up to Leadville no later than midnight, when them wine theaters will be fixing to close on a work shift change. Lobster shifters ain't big spenders."

So that was how they worked it. Leaving his McClellan saddle, his Winchester '73, and the rest of his field gear in his furnished digs, Longarm hopped the narrow guage for Leadville in his tobacco-tweed suit and pancaked black-coffee Stetson over his low-heeled army stovepipe boots and the Colt double action .44-40 he packed crossdraw on his left hip under the tail of his frock coat, trying for the overall effect of a tall, tanned, tough-looking cattle buyer or whiskey drummer.

Figuring he might do some crawling through dusty lofts, Longarm had packed clean but faded denim work duds with a wrecking bar in the gladstone bag he was packing, along with his shaving kit, change of socks, and such, including a fresh box of fifty Smith & Wesson .44-40 rounds. Prices up Leadville way were scandalous.

He detrained from the narrow guage at their north station a little after sundown to drift west along 7th Street to the north-south State. Most all the action in Leadville, save for mining, of course, took place along State betwixt 12th Street and Chestnut Street, which would have been 1st Street if they hadn't named it Chestnut after they'd laid out an Elm Street and a Front Street south of the

12

former 1st. Mining towns were inclined just to grow, like Topsy in *Uncle Tom's Cabin.*

Lusty Leadville had just growed since a bottomed-out gold strike in nearby California Gulch had been reconsidered by Uncle Billy Stevens, a prospector with enough experience to wonder what all that black shit clogging his sluice box might be. He got an assay man called Alonius Wood to test the inky sand with his blowpipe and it panned out as a lead-silver carbonate yielding forty ounces of silver to the ton of easily dug grit.

Within two years Stevens and Wood, along with others, had staked out nine rich claims in California Gulch alone, the richest being named after its odd ore, the Iron-Silver.

In no time the surrounding Carbonate, Fryer, and other hills were a honeycomb dug by delirious former gold miners who'd been mining one dollar in gold and throwing away ten in silver.

Near the center of all this hustle and bustle, on a rare patch of more level ground, a cluster of shanties called Slabtown came into being without plan but with obvious purpose. Somebody had to move a whole lot of raw ore on down to market.

The open warfare betwixt the Denver & Rio Grande and the Santa Fe railroads, shooting it out point-blank in the Royal Gorge to the south, had been the stuff of legends, with the Denver & Rio Grande the winner, hauling bulk down the Arkansas valley whilst the modest narrow-gauge LC&SRY served as the short line up from nearby Denver.

By this time Marshal Field and other Chicago big shots had horned in. Augustus Meyer and a Christian skinflint called Edwin Harrison had built a swamping smelter to reduce all that ore, with results so prosperous old Harrison had built a mansion and proposed they rename State Street after his illustrious self.

In the meanwhile, they'd renamed Slabtown as Leadville. Remote but rich, it now supported such divers establishments as the Tabor Opera House and his Silver Dollar Saloon, down through lesser legitimate theaters, less legitimate wine theaters, and thrice that many red-eye gut-bucket saloons.

Three oriental laundrymen from nearby Fairplay had been gunned down like dogs on the streets of Leadville, but a more tolerant eye had been turned on the likes of Poker Alice, a Cockney card sharp who looked a lot more like Calamity Jane than Calamity Jane had ever managed, or the more glamorous Belle Siddons, a noted Confederate spy who now ran Madam Vestal's Dance Hall on State Street.

Abner Prentiss had been captured in another whorehouse a few doors up.

Longarm knew Leadville's former resident pain in the ass, harmless-looking but deadly Doc Holliday, was down in the newer and even more remote silver camp of Tombstone at the moment. But he'd heard Soapy Smith was still around and hoped that wasn't true. Longarm and the charming, sly, and treacherous Jefferson Randolph Smith had a sort of friendly-unfriendly relationship due to the back-shooting bearded bastard's unwillingness to put up or shut up around a federal lawman with more important chores than compulsive crooks who refused to pull federal offenses.

Longarm met nobody he knew on the streets of Leadville in the gloaming. He checked into a hotel at State and 4th, handy to the Tabor Opera House and Silver Dollar Saloon owned by the same fortunate cuss, Horace "Silver Dollar" Tabor. He likely owned the Silver Bell Hotel as well. Longarm never asked as he checked in at higher rates than the Denver Palace charged, as if this smoky sprawl, high in the Rockies, was, for Gawd's sake, Paris, France.

Leaving his light baggage by the hired bed, Longarm

14

stepped out in the deserted hall to wedge a match stem under the bottom hinge before he locked the door and pocketed the key. As a well-traveled sport, he knew the room clerks downstairs would *rather* have guests packing their infernal keys instead of asking for 'em every time they went in or out.

Back outside he found State Street abustle in the gathering dusk as they changed shifts at the round-the-clock mines encircling the town. He was glad. The nitpicky rules called for a visiting lawman to pay a courtesy call on the town marshal. But he wanted half the off-duty lawmen in Lake County beating the bushes ahead of him about as bad as he wanted a dose of the clap. You were supposed to level with the local law when you went pussyfooting through their jurisdiction and he knew they were paid less than he was.

Any fool even guessing at a fortune hidden 'neath the floorboards above some wine theater would have little trouble finding it as long as nobody was giving him any trouble. The question before the house was: How many wine theaters might let him search their premises before the whole damned county heard what he was doing and spent all of five minutes figuring why? The arrest of a famous bank robber in a State Street house of ill repute had made every infernal newspaper west of the Big Muddy, and a couple back East.

After that he was faced with more choices than you could shake a wrecking bar at. The last time he'd counted, there'd been over a dozen such establishments within easy walking distance of that parlor house Prentiss had been holed up in. Others kept opening all the time. He needed some of what Billy Vail called the process of eliminating.

Having left his wrecking bar in his hired room for now, Longarm decided to begin at the end of the hunt for Abner Prentiss. He didn't need to consult his notes. He knew they'd arrested him at Madame Three Tits, just north of Madam Vestal's Dance Hall.

Though he was in no position to bet money on it, Longarm doubted Madame Three Tits was more than over-endowed, with the usual number inside her black-lace-and-red-satin bustier. You could see she'd been pretty, a spell back. But she had three chins to go with her sort of pouter-pigeon-encased-in-whalebone effect.

To say she and Longarm were old friends would have been to insult her professional approach to romance and Longarm's romantic approach to slap and tickle. But they'd brushed before and she remembered the tall, good-looking galoot as a lawman who'd treated her, if not with respect, with the common courtesy granted anyone but a convicted felon under the U.S. Constitution. So she sat him down in her combined crib and private office to pour her best stuff and ask how she or her girls might pleasure him most.

Longarm politely passed on her offer to fix him up with a new girl who really knew how to speak French, and got down to brass tacks by saying, "I spent some time with one of your other callers, the late Abner Prentiss, the night before they hanged him. Before you cloud up and rain all over me, I agree it ain't a federal offense to let a paying customer stay on, upstairs, as long as his money holds out."

Madame Three Tits pouted. "Lake County like to tore this place apart, searching for all that money he'd hidden somewheres else. I told them and told them he kept going out late at night for more to dole out, a few dollars at a time, to Cherry Poppins."

Longarm laughed despite himself and insisted, "You can't have any gal called Cherry Poppins working here or any other such place, no offense."

Madame Three Tits shrugged and replied, "None taken. Her professional name was bestowed upon her by satisfied customers who'd marveled at how any gal could still seem so young and innocent after servicing a whole drilling crew. Abner Prentiss seemed really taken by our Miss Cherry Poppins. Said she reminded him of some other gal he'd once known and . . . well, if the truth be told, he took to treating her more like a lady than a working girl. Used to get her gussied up so's he could take her out to supper and a show, as if they meant shit to one another."

Longarm swallowed the last of the Irish she'd served him before he suggested with a poker face he'd like a word with their Cherry Poppins.

So Madame Three Tits grunted herself off the chaise she'd been lolling on and went to her door to shout up the stairs for the world to hear, "Cherry Poppins! Front and center! Tell him to take it out and ask our new French girl to finish him off at no extra charge. For I got you a moose in pants down here who wants to shove eight inches up your ass!"

She turned to the thundergasted Longarm to confide, "It's fun to try, at least, to scare her. But, to tell the truth, I'm sure the sweet young thing could take *more* than eight inches up her ass and never bat her innocent-looking eyes!"

Chapter 3

It wasn't fair to the many harder-looking home girls. Cherry Poppins strode in bold as brass in a short chemise that barely covered her lap fuzz and Longarm *knew* she'd just been serving a paying customer in the cribs upstairs. But she still came across as a sweet sixteen who'd never been kissed.

She wore her straw-colored hair in pigtails and her big blue eyes regarded him with the innocence of a child, as Madame Three Tits teased, "This big moose is built too big for my old twat but we go back a ways and I told him you'd take it up the ass for him. So why don't you bend over and let me watch?"

To quote Victoria Regina, Longarm was not amused when the innocent-looking little thing calmy turned her shapely derriere to them, hoisted her chemise to expose her bare buttocks, and calmly bent over to assume the position suggested.

He said, "The madame was funning you, Miss Cherry. I'm the law. I was told the late Abner Prentiss singled you out for . . . special attention when he was staying here with you ladies a spell back."

Cherry Poppins straightened up and turned to face them

18

as she calmly replied, "Oh, him? He was all right, but sort of crazy. Paid me extra to play kid games with him. Didn't hurt me. Said he loved me when he got to slobbering in me, upstairs. But I sure got tired of his games by the time they came for him. Made me feel like *I* was sort of silly, too!"

Madame Three Tits chortled. "I knew he had to be queer for you when he paid me extra to single you out as his and his alone whilst he was here! What was his peculiar pleasure, French or Greek?"

Cherry Poppins shrugged her bare childish shoulders to reply, "He only wanted to fuck natural now and again, as if we were married up, for crying out loud. The queer part was the way he wanted me to put on all my duds and go out on the town with him in the gloaming. Said he'd always felt romantical around sunset and the tricky light made him feel safer out of doors."

Longarm was commencing to suspect he understood. He asked the just-plain-stupid but awesomely pretty little slut where a bank robber on the dodge had walked her in the gloaming.

She said, "Supper and a show, most times. He liked us both to gussy up like quality and sup in fancy restaurants with table linen and fine china. Chided me more than once about my table manners. I told him I'd always et that way and if he didn't fancy my eating peas with my knife he shouldn't order peas for me."

Longarm asked her to pray continue.

She said, "After dawdling over coffee and dessert longer than any kin *I* ever et with, he'd take me down the street to a wine theater he fancied and that was sort of tedious, too. Once we went to the opera house and that was more fun. They had horses and real camels up on the stage and everybody was dressed old-timey as they sung at one another in French. But old Abner liked the Carbonate Spa best and I had to sit there and sit there whilst the band played 'Who Shot Keyser's Dog' or 'The Gerry Owen.' "

She repressed a yawn and added, "Fat ladies in pink tights posed as wood nymphs and such on stage. One gal older than Madame Three Tits—no offense—came out dressed like them pictures of Miss Alice in Wonderland to sing about the fairies in the bottom of her garden. But when I asked Abner if he didn't want to take me home and fuck me he'd get all weepy-eyed and swear at me for breaking some spell. I had no idea what he was talking about. I still don't know what he was talking about! Do I look like a magic spell?"

Longarm soberly replied, "As a matter of fact you do. You were sort of filling in for long ago and faraway, Miss Cherry. You say the two of you always went to the Carbonate Spa after supper?"

She shook her braids and answered, "I said that seemed his favorite. There were other wine theaters we visited more than once, to my dismay. I told him I liked the opera house better. But somehow he hardly seemed to be listening to me."

Longarm said, "He wasn't. He was out on the town with somebody else, no offense. So I fear I may have to subject you to more torture."

She grinned and asked where he thought she couldn't take it.

He turned to Madame Three Tits and asked, "How much will it cost us to hire this substitute by the hour instead of the . . . usual?"

The canny old bawd cautiously asked if they were talking about clearing her skirts with Uncle Sam or getting her and her girls in deeper.

Longarm honestly replied, "County, state, and federal lawmen all agreed the late Abner Prentiss never cut you in on the proceeds of his last robbery. You were still alive when they caught him on these very premises, and Abner

Prentiss was not in the habit of leaving partners in crime alive. So we have you and your gals down as oddly innocent bystanders, already. I want to hire miss Cherry, here, to see if she can help me cut a sign along a literally dead man's trail."

Madame Three Tits said, "Cherry, go put on some duds. Try to dress like a lady. You've seen some in your travels."

The innocent-looking little whore shrugged and flounced out.

The older whore she worked for told Longarm, "I'll take care of her at no charge to you and Uncle Sam, Longarm. Ready for another drink?"

Longarm shook his head and replied, "Better save the thought for the street outside. Figures to be a drinking night as the two of us take in the sights along State Street whilst trying to avoid the attentions of State Street. Does Miss Cherry really enjoy her work in the cribs up yonder more than a night on the town?"

Madame Three Tits said, "She's out to become a legend in her own time. Somebody told her Lola Montez fucked two thousand men before they laid her to rest in New York City and our Cherry Poppins has vowed to top the notorious Lola before she retires alive and rich."

Longarm allowed she'd probably make it at the rate she was going.

Madame Three Tits confided, "I doubt it. She's awesomely stupid. Too stupid even to guess at how stupid that makes her. I don't see what that outlaw saw in her."

Longarm said, "He wasn't looking at her. He was staring through her at another young gal he told me about the night before he died. I feel sure he knew, deep down, what he was doing. But none of that matters to him now."

He set the empty shot glass aside as he continued, "What matters to *me* is following in his Leadville footsteps with the gal he stepped out with whilst he was hiding out up here. By pretending to be him, out on the town with the gal he was playing Let's Pretend with, I might just see . . . where they went."

"And if you don't?" she demanded.

Longarm shrugged and said, "I'll be no worse off than I was when I came in, and who knows, I might enjoy that song about the fairies in the bottom of that garden."

Madame Three Tits warned, "Be careful, Longarm. Cherry's dumb as a plank and inclined to flirt in public. I've told her she can't come to church with me and the other girls no more, having offered the preacher a blow job on the church steps. Like I said, a legend in her own time!"

It hadn't taken all that long for Cherry Poppins to get dressed. The effect when she sashayed in was thunder-gasting. She looked like some farmer's daughter gussied up for a night in town, sporting summer-weight calico skirts above high-button shoes of yellow kid with a perky straw boater pinned atop the blond hair she now wore in a schoolmarm's bun.

When Longarm suggested she might have overdone that schoolmarm outfit, Cherry Poppins asked, "What are you talking about? Ain't this the way ladies of fashion dress to sup in fancy restaurants down in Denver?"

Madame Three Tits laughed and silently mouthed, "Corn fed Iowa farm produce!" with her painted lips.

Longarm said she looked fine and suggested they get going. When he offered her his arm out on State Street she pouted and said she knew how to walk in high heels, durn it.

He settled for his left hand steering her by her right elbow and explained why as she tried to shrug him off.

She said that other queer duck, Abner, hadn't acted so citified. .

Longarm said, "He wasn't. He rode off to war from another farm and never studied manners much."

22

She pouted. "Who were *you* brung up by, fancy city dudes?"

He said, "Not hardly. I'm just an old-West, by-God Virginia boy my ownself. But playing by the rules saves bother and having others staring at you in public. A gent walking a lady by her arm as he shields her skirts from street-splashes with his own pants strikes other gents in passing that they are *together* and she ain't *unescorted*, see?"

"You mean they're liable to take you for my *beau* if I cling to your arm like a fucking vine?" she demurely asked.

He allowed that was about the size of it. So she latched on to his elbow and as they passed a pool hall she told the youths loitering in the doorway, "I'm with this good-looking cuss and we're on our way to a set-down supper at a fancy restaurant!"

One of the punks laughed and said, "Well, good on you, then!" But Longarm let it pass as likely harmless in meaning, if not intent.

When Cherry Poppins pointed out the place calling itself La Petite Rose across State Street as the late Abner's favorite beanery, Longarm took her there for supper. He was sincerely hungry by that hour.

The menu was half fake-French, but the entrees ran to steak and potatoes served by a fat Irish waitress. So when Cherry Poppins started to order the same Longarm hushed her with a warning look and murmured, "The lady is supposed to tell the gent what she wants for supper so's he can order for both of them."

She said, "I don't want no brussels sprouts. I like the string beans they serve here better."

Longarm asked if she meant with steak and spuds, and how rare she liked her steak. She told him she never et nothing but steak and spuds and preferred the beef to still be bleeding.

23

The waitress shot Longarm a disgusted look as he ordered for them both. As she left for the kitchen Cherry Poppins giggled and told him, "She thinks you're a dirty old man messing with my innocent ass. How come the gent gets to order? Is that supposed to make him look bigger and stronger than the gal he's messing with?"

Longarm said, "I suspect such manners were worked out over time to save time and avoid confusion. Things go smoother when it's understood in advance that the gent walks closer to the curb and lets the lady go first through the doors he holds open for her."

She asked why things had to be that way.

He said, "They don't. Indians and Chinese, I understand, think just as highly of their womenkind as they walk *ahead* of them. In the case of the Indians, the man goes first so as to spot danger first and deal with it before the lady gets to it. The Chinese can speak for their own selves but I suspect their reasoning is similar. In any case it ain't so much who does what as it is both parties know the form to *start out* with and don't have to sign a treaty before they walk down the street together, see?"

She said, "I guess. Would you like to order me some of that apple pie with ice cream for dessert?"

When he ordered pie à la mode for the both of them, Cherry Poppins laughed at him for putting on airs.

He said, "It ain't putting on airs to order in French in a French restaurant, as long as you know what you're ordering. If I didn't know how to say pie à la mode I'd be putting on airs by trying. There's a saying about doing as the Romans do when you go to Rome. It may strike some as putting on airs. Others feel it's a good way to keep Romans from staring at you, and it ain't polite to wave at other men through a restaurant window when you're having a set-down supper with another man entire."

She looked innocent as she lowered her flirty hand back beside her plate to explain, "I wouldn't want regular customers saying I've been putting on hoity-toity airs and both those old boys have fucked me in the recent past."

Longarm studied on that through coffee and dessert. Madame Three Tits had warned him Cherry Poppins had nothing betwixt her ears but a pretty face, and *smart* gals with pretty faces could get a man in a whole lot of trouble on State Street after dark.

He knew, if he had to, he could mosey from one wine theater to another without her, just as Abner Prentiss could have, as a stranger looking for action, stag, to the regulars. Most of the tables in those wine theaters would be occupied by parties or couples, with the stags along the bar where the night manager could keep closer tabs on them.

As they finished their coffee and dessert, Longarm resisted the temptation to lecture a wayward kid, born and raised as trash, on how a well-brought-up farm gal, for Pete's sake, was expected to act on the street with her damned duds on.

As they left the French restaurant she said she wanted him to take her to the opera house down by 3rd and State. He said that Carbonate Spa, closer to 7th, was where they'd be starting. She called him a mean old shit but clung to his arm as they crossed the crowded State Street to catty-corner weaving through the carriages and drays.

Once you got inside, the Carbonate Spa looked more like a wine theater than a plain saloon because a trio was playing "Aura Lee" in front of the asbestos curtain illuminated by stage lights to advertise patent cures for alcoholism, cancer, consumption, and all forms of social diseases. The floor wasn't too crowded yet, so when Longarm bet a waitress two bits she couldn't find them a table up front he lost and Cherry Poppins said she'd never sat that close to the stage before.

They'd just settled in with the pitcher of wine, or leastwise cider, he'd ordered and it looked as if the show was about to commence when a mining man seated with four others at a nearby table called out, "Well, shit and be damned if that don't look like Cherry Poppins from Madame Three Tits's place! Stand up and take a bow, Cherry Poppins! Bow the other way so's the boys can see your ass!"

Cherry Poppins blushed for the first time since Longarm had laid eyes on her and whispered, "I want to go home. Or back where I belong, leastways!"

Longarm said, "We won't be the ones leaving, Miss Cherry," as he rose to his full height to face the pretty little nitwit's tormentors with a smile.

It was not a friendly smile as Longarm asked in a tone as cold as the keel of a Viking ship, "Would you care to rephrase what you just said to the lady I happen to be escorting, or would you care to fill your fist with some hardware?"

Chapter 4

All four of them got to their feet. Two were almost as tall as Longarm. Not a one was a shrimp. Then a saner head soothed, "Old Ralph, here, ain't armed, mister, and I'm sure what he just said was only in jest."

Before Longarm could answer a whirlwind of white apron over shiny black taffeta skirts with mesh stockings was between their tables and barking, "That's enough, and we're not running that sort of place!"

Longarm had just figured out she was the boss waitress who'd told their younger waitress to seat them when she pointed at him to snap, "I was listening. You're in the right, but shut up and sit down and let me handle this!"

Longarm said, "Yes'm," and sat down.

Cherry Poppins whispered to him, "That's the Powerful Patricia. Never cross her nor call her Pat!"

From his lower vantage point, looking up at all five foot nine of her, Longarm saw the Powerful Patricia's bare arms were well-muscled for a gal's and her jaw was too manly for her otherwise handsome face. After that she seemed about thirty with the milk-white skin and jet-black hair that hailed from odd corners of the British Isles. She had no accent as she told the out-of-line mining men,

"You four, over to the table our Margie has cleared for you near the wall, unless you would rather just pay your tabs and go!"

One of the mining men protested, "Old Ralph meant no harm, Miss Patricia."

To which she replied with a firmer set to her jaw, "None of you would be here, now, if we didn't all know Ralph Trevor as a well-paid Cousin Jack without a brain to call his own and I am not going to ask the four of you to move your asses again!"

So, seeing they were on their feet, they moved their asses out of earshot across the floor as other tables were already crowding up for the expected stage show.

The trio struck up a cakewalk and the curtain rose to reveal two white couples wearing blackface and gussied up like nobody, white or black, had ever gussied up for a real promenade along what seemed a beach resort where grass-green waves stood frozen forever against a skyline of robins-egg blue. One of the cakewalking gals seemed to have a game leg she had to favor, but they were trying.

And Cherry Poppins was crying. Real tears rolled down her cheeks as she sat there prim and propper, trying not to let her feelings show.

Longarm reached across the table to take one hand as he soothed, "It's over. Even his pals saw he was in the wrong and everyone else here is on your side."

She blubbered, "I know! You're all treating me like a fucking lady and I really did take that Cornishman in my ass, and two others off his drill crew, sandwich style. That's when the girl gets on top with one cuss in her pussy and—"

"I know about sandwich style," he cut in, adding, "A famous opera star is said to like it no other way. But nobody talks dirty to her when she's out on the town with an escort."

The Powerful Patricia came back to their table, bending

low so as not to interfere with the stage show as she said, "Them gentlemen at that other table have asked us to serve you some real wine as a token of their respect. We got champagne if you want it. If you'd allow me to advise you, order our Rhineland May wine from New York State. Some champagne sparkles natural whilst other brands are fizzed with carbolic acid that ain't good for your teeth."

Longarm allowed in that case they'd have the May wine. He'd forgotten until a regular waitress brought it to their table in an ice bucket how odd May wine could taste to anyone who'd never had any before.

Cherry Poppins sipped and exclaimed, "Jesus H. Christ! What's in this shit?"

Longarm said, "Woodruff. That's an herb as grows in May back in the old countries. They toss some in the white grape mash to remind us of Maytime in the Black Forest where they carve the cuckoo clocks."

She sipped again and decided, "It does sort of taste like it smells back home in the greenup. More like fresh meadow grass than woods, though. How did you ever learn all the shit you know, Custis?"

He said, "Mostly by reading, I confess. I ain't never watched anybody make May wine. I only read about it in a travel book about the Black Forest. I often wind up reading alone in bed at night near the end of the month when the pocket jingle runs low."

She said, "I never learned to read. Abner could read, and recite from the Good Book. Sitting in this very place, at another table, he recited to me about my tits being doves."

Longarm nodded and said, "From the 'Song of Solomon.' Never did figure out what all them personal remarks about a lady's build was doing in the Good Book. But, no matter. He was telling another lady entire how grand he still thought she was. Did he ever up and . . . leave you

29

setting alone in this or any other wine theater, Miss Cherry?"

She asked, "You mean to go take a piss? I reckon. You men piss more than us girls and it's a blessing you get to do so standing up."

He started to say he was talking about longer intervals. He doubted she'd been paying that much attention. The two couples in blackface cakewalked off stage and a cuss with a black cape and a gal with her knees exposed by her shocking outfit came out to perform magic tricks.

Knowing everybody was supposed to be staring at the assistant gal's knees instead of the magician's hands, Longarm excused himself to slip away from their table as if heeding a call of nature.

The Carbonate Spa was floor-planned the usual Roman basilica way, with cast-iron pillars to either side of the central space supporting the clerestory windows under the main roof span, with the bar filling one side aisle and the other leading backstage and beyond to their outdoor shit houses.

Longarm boldly strode out the back door and across the dark yard to strike a match and find the door meant for gents. He pissed inside in the dark, shook the dew off the lily, and buttoned up to head back inside, innocent as any other pisser visiting a wine theater. Facing the back door and rear windows now, he saw nobody seemed to be paying him any mind out in the yard. He got out his pocket knife and opened the screwdriving blade as he moved casual as anything.

He knew they'd lock that back door after closing time. He knew the nigh pickpoof brand of lock they'd installed in the heavy oaken door as well. Holding the door ajar as if lounging there for a last whiff of the cool mountain air, when the wind wasn't blowing from those big round-the-clock smelters, Longarm quietly loosened one retaining screw of the latch plate. It was out of reach once the door

30

was shut, meant to retain the drum of the patent lock from twisting if and when you applied twisting pressure from outside. He intended to come back in the wee small hours with his wrecking bar, in his work duds, before he'd need to unscrew the fool lock and just reach a finger in to unlatch the fool door.

As he sensed somebody else on his way to the shit house he slipped the unfolded knife in a side pocket and let the door shut behind him as he headed back to his table.

The Powerful Patricia blocking his path demanded, "All right. So what are you, another lawman or another treasure hunter?"

Longarm tried to sound puzzled as he tried, "Which would you like best for me to be, Miss Patricia?"

She said, "Let's not shit each other. I was on to your game as soon as you came in with that bank robber's favorite whore. You sure picked a swell guide to lead you along State Street in his footsteps. It was sweet of you to stand up for her like that, but any man out to defend the honor of Cherry Poppins has Don Quixote beat as a gallant fool!"

Longarm sighed and said, "I have noticed Miss Cherry seems to have a lot of . . . admirers in this town."

The Powerful Patricia said, "A tough town. As tough a town as you'll find north or south of the border. A town where a man can get himself killed just for wearing his hair in a pigtail or snoring too loud in his own hotel room, and you want to traipse around defending a famous Leadville whore against personal remarks from satisfied customers?"

Longarm chuckled at the picture and replied, "What can I tell you? Ain't no windmills up here in Leadville for a fool in rusty armor to tilt at. I was hoping to attract less attention down this way with a woman on my arm. After that, Miss Cherry was the woman Abner Prentiss was

31

with, out front, on all those other occasions."

The Powerful Patricia said, "Carry her home to Madame Three Tits and come back in an hour, if I'm *in*, that is."

Longarm knew better than to ask in what. He said, "I reckon it's time to cut the cards, Miss Patricia. I'd be Deputy U.S. Marshal Custis Long, out to recover fifty grand the late Abner Prentiss didn't have on him when they arrested him at Miss Cherry Poppins's place of employment. If I write you up for an assist on the recovery you stand to collect no more than five grand nor less than one grand as your finder's fee. Do you still want in?"

She said, "My God, you're *him*! The one they call Longarm, and of *course* I want in, if you're talking about my getting away free and clear with my share and nobody ever pestering me about it."

He nodded and said, "No way the law can ever pester an honest citizen about her own money, once she's earned it. That tax on one's personal fortune collected by Queen Victoria is another reason for us to celibrate our revolution. Beats me how the Lime Juicers put up with such notions. You're sure you can get off early if I carry Miss Cherry Poppins back to her house of ill repute? What do you aim to tell your boss?"

The Powerful Patricia said, "I *am* my own boss. As a part owner I ride herd over the help to see the joint's run right. But a thousand dollars free and clear is more than me and my partners will have to share by the end of the week and . . . well, having you defending my *own* honor the length of State Street after dark sounds like more fun!"

So they shook on it and Longarm went back to their table to gently ask Cherry Poppins to finish her glass because he was taking her home.

She protested, "It's still early and I *like* being treated like a fucking lady! Don't you want me to show you the other places me and Abner visited?"

32

He started to burn that bridge behind him, but decided a rain check made more sense. The Powerful Patricia knew her way around the streets of Leadville better. Cherry Poppins had been there at times Abner Prentiss might have behaved oddly. He hated it when they made him go over the same ground again and again, but there were times the only other choice was giving up.

Paying the waitress and leaving her a decent tip, Longarm took Cherry Poppins back to her whorehouse, where Madame Three Tits seemed surprised, and suspicious, asking Longarm, "What happened? Did she fuck up?"

Longarm shook his head and said, "Matter of fact, Miss Cherry did a swell job. Thanks to her I met up with others who might be able to tell me more about old Abner than Miss Cherry here found out in the short time she knew him."

Other denizens of the establishment were peeking out of the woodwork now as Cherry Poppins declaimed, "We went to a fancy French restaurant and et pie in the mud and then we drank fancy mayfly wine that smelled like new-mowed hay, and when some customer I fucked one time started up with me, my Egg Scott here made him take it back and . . . Oh, shit, it felt so *good* to be treated like a fucking lady!"

Longarm said, "Aw, mush. I got to go now. I'll get back to you so's we can settle up before I leave town, Madame Three Tits."

He left before any of those whores asked him to walk on water or raise the dead. He'd eliminated one thing about Abner Prentiss, now. No bank robber treacherous enough to gun his own sidekicks and ride the way nobody should have expected him to ride would have had the loot on him whilst taking his substitute truelove out on the town. That brush with Cherry Poppins's loose-lipped customers had only been a sample of the sort of attention a whore's escort attracted. Old Abner had been indulging himself in romantic daydreams with Cherry Poppins. He'd been more discreet when he'd hidden the money and he'd likely had a good laugh, later, sipping wine with the pretty little nitwit under the fifty grand he'd hidden earlier.

Prentiss had said right out that the money was betwixt joists above a wine theater. He hadn't said *which one* before his time ran out. There were close to a score of such establishments along State Street alone.

So he turned on the steps to go back up and ask Cherry Poppins if she and old Abner had visited any wine theater *off* State Street.

She said, "All but one were on State. We did go to this fancy place near Chestnut and Pine. The Organ Lye, I think they called it. It had elk racks all over the wall and they served a wine they called virgin's milk, the sassy things. Everybody sang in High Dutch and I didn't care for it much. So he never took me back there. Why do you ask?"

Longarm said, "Eliminating. I suspect 'Lorelei' was the name you were reaching for if they serve *Liebfraumilch* and entertain in Dutch."

Cherry Poppins shrugged and decided, "If you say so."

Bidding them all a fond farewell, Longarm took his time getting on down to the Carbonate Spa. He didn't see the Powerfull Patricia when he went in to stand by the bar. He didn't say anything, but the barkeep told him Miss Patricia would be down in a minute.

It was more like three, but worth the wait. When she joined Longarm at the bar for a State Street promenade the Powerful Patricia's hair was pinned up differently under a fashionable hat with a half-veil and if that summer frock hadn't been put together in Paris, France, some other dressmaker had busted her guts trying for such a fashionable effect. In sum, the tall athletic brunette could

34

have passed for some railroad baron's play-pretty slumming out West.

The only thing she couldn't have passed for was sweet sixteeen and never been kissed. Poor little Cherry Poppins had that all sewed up along State Street that night.

Chapter 5

Being in the business, the Powerful Patricia knew the Lorelei as a rival establishment run by Dutchmen down to
the far end of town. So she suggested they start there and
work their way north until they made it back to her neck
of the woods.

Leaving her on the walk out front, Longarm stepped
out on the unpaved street to flag down a cruising hansom
for the half mile ride to Chestnut and Pine.

Once they were there, Longarm could see the Lorelei
didn't work so good. But he was still playing his own
cards close to his vest. The greeter was a portly gent with
a walrus mustache and a sauerkraut accent who recognized the Powerful Patricia and treated them as honored
guests. A singing waiter in those short leather pants
showed them to a table near the stage and confided with
a snicker that the house wine translated as virgin's milk.

He was full of shit, but nobody liked a know-it-all, so
Longarm never said he'd been assured at Kramer's Beer
Garden in Denver that you translated *Liebfraumilch* as
"loving wife" or "bride's milk," and in either case it was
a light Rhine wine, a tad sweet to Longarm's taste.

As Cherry Poppins had observed earlier, the walls all

around, made to look half timbered with stucco and strips of sepia pine, held rack after rack of Rocky Mountain elk horn, meant to be red deer from, say, the *Rothaargebirge*, and likely close enough, both species being related way back when, if you believed Professor Darwin.

The Powerful Patricia opined they'd spent too much on a place so far off the beaten track. Longarm asked if it wasn't true they paid less rent over that way as he stared morosely up at a vaulted ceiling.

Most business establishments in most Western towns occupied much the same sized twenty-five- or fifty-by-hundred-foot lots, with easy-to-erect balloon frame or bolted-together cast-iron kit the preferred construction. Behind the squared-off false fronts they presented to the street the favored roofing was tar papered or corrugated iron in peaked or flatter shed form. Most peaked roofs naturally had room up yonder for attics or garrets, and Prentiss had suggested he'd hidden the money under the flooring of such a space.

The Lorelei offered no such space. It's peaked roof was held up yonder by exposed truss timbers, as if the place were some for-Gawd's-sake Bavarian barn. But what the hell, the show was about to begin and he wasn't ready to tell the Powerful Patricia just what they might be looking for.

A whole family dressed up like Alpine peasants proceeded to sing tuneful but unintelligible songs from their old country as many of the other customers waved their glasses and sang along in Dutch.

There was a lot of that going around, ever since Bismarck had come to power and started drafting farm boys into his Kaiser's Prussian army, and the Know-Nothing party kept bitching that at the rate things were going the English-speaking real Americans would soon be drowned out by all the infernal Dutch and Irish that just kept coming by the boatload.

Since neither of them cared to sing along in Dutch, the Powerful Patricia felt free to ask Longarm why a bank robber off a Kansas farm might want to squire a whore off an Iowa farm to such a place.

Longarm said, "He was trying to seem wordly to the gal he'd left behind him. Miss Cherry said he was prone to recite the 'Song of Solomon' to her, too. He had money to spend and when you picture the two of them dressed to the nines instead of for riding, it's easier to see how our murdersome but sentimental bank robber was able to pass for a sort of sissified townsmen for a spell. I'm still working on how your Leadville law wound up arresting him *indoors* after he'd gotten away with visiting so many public places with the notorious Cherry Poppins."

He took a sip of *Liebfraumilch* and observed, "You were on the money when you said I was looking for trouble in her company and the late Abner Prentiss was smaller than me. Yet they never attracted all that much attention, and how do you eliminate that?"

The Powerful Patricia said, "That's easy. You *called* that Cousin Jack and his drill crew when he passed that remark. Speaking from my observation post at the Carbonate Spa, most men pretend they don't hear such remarks unless the pest comes right over and grabs their gal by her hair."

Longarm glanced up at the vaulted ceiling and replied, "Prentiss was armed and dangerous when they arrested him. He killed two pals in cold blood on his way up here from Camp Weld. Back-shot them as the three of them were fording the South Platte right after the robbery. Abner Prentiss, in sum, was not a sissy."

The tall, athletic brunette smiled wistfully across the table at him to remark, "Most men don't consider it sissified to avoid a fight at four-to-one odds, Custis. Most of us girls don't expect you to, even when you've been reciting love poems at us from the Good Book and, after

38

that, in spite of the romantic games he was playing with a notorious woman of the town, he surely knew it was a *game*, not worth a shoot-out in a public place!"

Longarm said, "I reckon. Funny how he got away with escorting Miss Cherry around in public, only to be arrested at her place of business."

The Powerful Patricia said, "I can answer that. But let's get out of here unless you think there's a buried treasure on the premises."

Longarm said it hardly seemed likely, the interior being so barnlike and simple. As they rose he left some change on the table and asked her on the way out if he'd tipped about right.

She said, "A little on the cowboy side. We in the business feel the customers who tip less than ten percent are cheap while those tipping more than fifteen are cowboys. You shouldn't have left those two pennies. Makes it look as if you didn't calculate, and of course when you *do* so it's insulting to leave less than a nickel, even when your bill is no more than two bits."

They'd agreed in advance to ride down to Chestnut and Pine and work their way back to her place on foot. As they walked over to State Street, with her long legs in step with his own, Longarm asked her what she'd meant about the surprise arrest at the parlor house Abner Prentiss had holed up in.

She said, "They were tipped off, of course. We've just agreed the fool was escorting a notorious hooker with a known business address all over Leadville. One of the arresting officers drinks at the bar in my place. He bragged how they's taken the federal want without a struggle and searched the premises high and low for the loot. Until you came along I'd frankly thought they'd *found* it. If you've been reading our *Herald Democrat* you know what they say about the glorified bully boys enforcing such laws as we have up this way."

Longarm started to observe that the money had never been recovered. Then he reconsidered but didn't think it proper to question the honesty of his fellow lawmen before he'd made sure they weren't the crooks she'd just accused them of being. It happened. A brazen road agent known as Henry Plummer had been elected *sheriff* by other mining men up Montana way.

The Golden Ingot Wine Theatre near State and 2nd had a low flat ceiling under its peaked roof. Longarm waited until they'd been there a spell before he excused himself to go prowling out back.

The Powerful Patricia didn't comment until he'd done that three more times in as many stops up State Street. When he rejoined her in the Bighorn after doctoring the back door with his screwdriver blade she demurely asked, "Have you got the clap, Custis?"

To which he could only reply, "I don't think so. I sure hope I don't. Are we talking about my occasional visits to the facilities, Miss Patricia?"

She said, "We are. And they haven't been occasional. They've been a lot closer to constant. I naturally took a good pee before we left the Carbonate Spa less than an hour ago. So I haven't had to go once whilst you've left me for protracted spells at every damned table we sat down at so far. So if you don't have the clap, what on earth *are* you suffering from, down yonder?"

He smiled sheepishly and confessed, "Nothing. Knock wood. I've been snooping around like a mouse in the woodwork, looking for a likely place to cache a sack of gold. We know Prentiss and his trusting pals lit out with mostly twenty-dollar double eagles and some silver certificates. So we're talking about a bundle the size of feed sack but way heavier. A load a man on the dodge would want to hide out of sight the first chance he got."

The big brunette frowned thoughtfully and asked, "But what makes you think he hid it in one of these wine the-

40

aters, Custis? He'd have ridden through miles of open range and aspen forest before he ever got up here to Leadville. Wouldn't he have been smarter to cache it somewhere out in the hills before he rode on into town?"

Longarm cocked a brow to ask, "Cache a sack of gold down a rabbit hole or under a rock in *mining country*, Miss Patricia? There ain't a lonesome line rider nor sheep herder within a day's ride of here who's never heard the true tale of the two prospectors drinking in the shade of a lonesome pine who finished the jug and decided they might as well dig where they'd been drinking."

She sighed and said, "Hook and Risch, grubstaked with a few dollars' worth of supplies by a Slabtown storekeeper called Horace Tabor. I see what you mean. Digging by guess and by God resulted in that famous Little Pittsburgh, and Silver Dollar Tabor was off and running with his share in a strike producing twenty thousand dollars a week. Became a millionaire twice over by exchanging his interests in *that* claim for a million in cash and mining shares floated by that railroad baron, Dave Moffat. So you just never know what you'll find if you dig most anywhere in the hills all around."

She sipped her wine and asked, "But what makes you so sure he hid the loot in one of these wine theaters and not under, say, a stable or a cigar store?"

Longarm said, "He *told* me he hid the money in a wine theater. How come they all serve wine, by the way? What's wrong with whiskey and beer?"

She said, "Whiskey drunks are harder to handle and beer sells too cheap to pay for serious entertaining. What do you mean he told you he hid the money in a wine theater? Are you trying to disillusion me about our Leadville law? The money *wasn't* hidden in that whorehouse?"

Longarm said, "If it had been we might not be having this conversation. I was awarded the dubious pleasure of spending the last hours before his hanging with the unfortunate cuss. He only opened up at the last, and the hangman thought he was only stalling for time. Men about to hang are inclined to do that. So I only got a few words about wine theaters being swell for hiding your money before they boosted him up them thirteen steps on me."

She whistled and said, "I'll bet that hurt! You, not him, to feel you were getting so warm just before the game was called. You don't know *where* in any particular wine theater he said he'd hidden the money?"

"Nope," Longarm lied. "Wouldn't have to visit so many of 'em if I knew what I was doing in any of 'em. So that's how come you've been spending so much time at the tables alone. I ain't found a dime of the missing money, so far, if that's any comfort to you."

She sighed and said, "All this talk about having to piss has my own plumbing acting up. Have I got time to go before it's time to go on up to the next joint?"

He said, "The ladies' facilities are to your left out back. I'll settle up whilst you do what you gotta do."

She did and he had by the time she returned, and they went on up past the opera house, where the three-sheets out front announced they were fixing to replace the opera *Fra Diavalo* with *The Flower Girls of Paris*.

And so it went, from one wine theater to the next, skipping the more plentiful saloons, dance halls, pool rooms, and such, because the soon-to-be-late Abner Prentiss hadn't said he'd hidden the money in such places. The Powerful Patricia was a good sport about sitting alone a lot and made his prowling easier because she was known to be in the business and hence unlikely to be sipping house wine with a known burglar.

Longarm felt sort of shitty as he played his cards closer to his vest than he was letting on. The suggestions she'd made along the way about handy places to cache money bags had been good ones. So it wasn't her fault she was so far off the mark. But having no pressing need to tell

42

her he knew where to look, later on, alone, once he'd fixed a lot of back doors to facilitate a little unconstitutional pussyfooting, he didn't tell her. He knew she'd find tedious all that shit about getting fixed up with a proper search warrant, once he knew where to declare he'd found the money. Most *men* did, and she was a woman.

He knew there was no way he could hope to sneak-search all the joints they visited that night in one night. But by the time he got her back to the Carbonate Spa he'd fixed back doors all along State Street in a way to unlock them with his trigger finger.

He was a big man, she was a big woman, and neither had sipped half the wine they'd had to order along the way as they'd worked their way up State Street. But they'd had to order at a whole lot of tables and he had to steady the Powerful Patricia as she tripped on the plank walk out front of the Carbonate Spa and muttered, "Got to fire that fucker I told to fix that loose plank. For he never fixed it and somebody's fixing to bust a fucking *neck* out here!"

She pointed at a private entrance on the far side of the stained-glass front windows and said, "I gotta go inside and glare good night at the help. Why don't you go on up to my quarters and I'll be up in a minute to brew us some coffee. We both need coffee bad, you wine-swilling Don Quixote! Gwan upstairs and wait for me and may-haps we'll find that pot of gold at the end of the rainbow and . . . Custis?"

He answered, "What?"

She said, "I hope you weren't fibbing to me, before, when I asked you if you had the clap."

He soberly replied, "I don't. I can show you, if you like."

She soberly replied, "Fuck the help. They can scare themselves. Let's get up them stairs, Don Quixote!"

Chapter 6

There were times to ask idle questions and there were times to help a lady out of her clothes.

The powerful long legs of the Powerful Patricia hugged him tight against her firm torso and muscular tits as her warm wet innards bit down and sucked on his old organ grinder like a half-weaned calf and he believed her when she sobbed she hadn't been getting any lately and she'd forgotten how good it felt down yonder.

So a good time was had by all, twice in a row, without any need to change positions and, even better, once he'd made her come a couple of times the big brunette neither accused him of rape nor pretended to feel ashamed of herself for liking it that much.

They were sharing a three-for-a-nickel smoke, propped up on pillows against her headboard, when Longarm got around to asking how come she was still calling him her Don Quixote.

She draped a shapely naked leg over his bare knee as she asked if he didn't recall how Don Quixote had named a village harlot his lady fair, Dulcenia, and defended her honor all dressed up in armor.

He snorted. "I wasn't defending her honor. I was defending my own honor. Nobody who thinks much of a man insults the woman he's with in front of her and others."

She said, "Let's not quibble. I was there. I could see you were the sort of gentleman a hard-up working girl's reputation would be safe with. So you never had a chance."

Longarm laughed and asked, "Am I to understand that all that help you gave to me this evening was offered with this vile abuse of my fair white body in mind?"

She purred, "I haven't even begun to abuse you, yet. Wait until I get my second wind. Did you really think I gave a shit about any hidden treasure that's already been found, if it was ever there at all?"

He asked, "You still think your town law's been searching ahead of me, Miss Dulcenia? I thought we'd established I was the one the late Abner Prentiss told about that wine theater."

She shrugged her naked shoulder against his bare ribs and replied, "Maybe. They arrested him months ago and who's to say what he said to whom as he was passed from one lawman to the next on his way to those thirteen steps?"

Longarm sighed and said, "It does take months to try and hang a cuss, don't it? But had he told someone else along the way about hiding the loot in some wine theater—"

"He'd had months to search every one in Leadville from top to bottom, and never gotten around to telling anyone else what he found if he'd already found it! We've agreed you're more idealistic than a heap of knight errants who've ridden to *this* fair maiden's rescue!"

He filed away her suggestion about crooked lawmen for later, when he made his required courtesy call on the local law. He felt no call to tell anyone he'd pretty well eliminated the Carbonate Spa for any late-night prowling, now that he'd been *invited* up under its pitched roof as they were closing for the night down below. He'd established whilst undressing them both for bed that the Powerful Patricia dwelt alone above the main floor to keep an eye on the premises lest some sneaky son of a bitch creep in downstairs. Her quarters consisted of a kitchen, bath, sitting room, and bedroom lined up as a railroad flat along a scrootchy hall with storage space farther in under the eaves. That, two unoccupied guest rooms, and a storage attic toward the back offered plenty of floorboards a bank robber on the dodge might have pried up. But she'd have noticed had Abner Prentiss been staying there, and she said only one of her married business partners used the far guest room, now and again, for entertaining ladies other than his wife.

The Powerful Patricia sniffed and said, "I've warned him not to ever carry on like so in the very next room. It's not that I'm a prude—you know I'm not a prude— but it's not fair to introduce a business partner to your wife and then screw other women she'd have to lie about. Do you think I'm a prude, Don Quixote?"

He soberly assured her, "You ain't a prude. He's acting crude, fair Dulcenia. I know the feeling. Had to tell off a fellow deputy about his abuse of our friendship when he asked me to cover for him and his other woman after his wife had served me a swell meal at their place. I told him I was not about to take part in one of those French bedroom farces dashing all about like a red-faced fool when I didn't get to fornicate with either of the she-male actresses."

The big brunette laughed and said, "That's exactly the way I feel about covering up for a man I'd never care to sleep with, whether I liked his poor wife or not!"

Longarm asked about her other business partner. She said, "He never stays here at night. He's never said how he gets along with his own wife, or even if he's really

46

married to her. I don't know anything about his personal life. That's the kind of business partner I admire. Business is business. I learned a long time ago not to screw around with anybody I did business with!"

Longarm braced himself. But the Powerful Patricia didn't dredge up all the men in her past who'd used and abused her. So he was feeling sincerely fond of his Dulcenia as they sniffed out the smoke so he could tilt her windmills some more with the lance she'd gotten up for him again whilst humming a French tune.

By lamplight all that alabaster flesh she had to offer, dog style, made her invite to spend the whole night mighty tempting. But knowing he didn't have near enough darkness left as it was, he warned her, around 2:00 A.M., that both their reputations might be under observation and suggested it might be best if he was at his hotel downtown if and when any local lawman called on him first.

He explained, "It's considered common courtesty for a visiting lawman to call on the resident law during regular business hours. I don't know whether the Leadville law knows I came in this evening or not. If they've heard I'm in town they might or might not await my formal call. If your suspicions about that fifty grand should prove correct, somebody with a guilty conscience could be squirming like a wiggle-worm caught by the sunrise on a flagstone walk. Be best if the desk clerk at my hotel had me in my hired bed, official, tonight."

She sighed and said, "It's sweet of you to worry about my reputation. But why don't we shower together before you get dressed?"

He said that sounded swell, then thought back and asked, "How come you got indoor plumbing up here and holes in the ground for customers out back?"

She said, "I've only recently been able to squat and drop it like a lady up here. We have running water piped to the bar down below as well. We'll worry about the

47

dressing rooms and crappers out back when he can *afford* more modern plumbing. Considering they call this town Leadville, and it's shipping more lead by far than silver, one would think the infernal lead pipes we have to send away for were made of gold! But come on, I'll scrub your back and you can scrub my back with it in me whilst I show off my modern plumbing!"

It was a good thing the bar right under them had closed for the night, he decided, as the Powerful Patricia pounded the walls of her booth and stomped her bare heels on the wet tiles. Longarm wound up stomping some, himself, by the time they'd finished *scrubbing* each other up there.

It was after 3:00 by the time he got back to his hotel and, once he got there, the night clerk said he'd had callers, more than once, wearing badges and acting more pissed each time they failed to find him in residence.

Longarm decided to put off any further night crawling as he made sure his hired room was empty, got undressed some more, and considered just how much pussyfooting might be involved.

As of that evening, Leadville supported seven smelters and three undertaking parlors. Of it's eighty-two saloons only a score qualified as wine theaters, and as they'd prowled, Longarm had been able to see a third of them wouldn't fit the story Prentiss had told about floorboards above the main hall. Some, like the Lorelei, had vaulted ceilings. Others, like the Carbonate Spa, had occupied quarters above the main floor. That still left seven or eight. Mayhaps nine. Sometimes you just couldn't tell without climbing on up.

There was nothing he could do about any of them now, and for some reason he was feeeling a tad tuckered. So he dimmed the lamp, hit the sack, and the next thing he knew it was daylight and somebody seemed to be hammering on his door with a nine-pound sledge.

"I'm Jesus H. Christ *coming*, and knock it off!" Longarm groaned as he rolled his bare feet to the floor. But his imperious early-morning visitor just pounded harder above his muttered curses as he rose, naked, knotted a hotel towel around his waist, and, just in case, hauled his six-gun from its bedpost holster with one hand as he rubbed sleep from his eyes with the other on his way to the Gawd-damned door.

He'd been expecting another lawman, or somebody out to kill him, so they were both surprised when Longarm opened the door in the startled face of a bitty schoolmarm, or a brown-haired gal of about twenty-five in a summer-weight frock of polka-dot gingham she filled just right.

She said, "Oh! You're naked and pointing a gun at me!"

To which he could only reply, "When you're right you're right, and what in thunder were you pounding with just now, ma'am?"

She held up the brass handle of her parasol with a pencil and shorthand pad gripped in the same small fist and said, "You never answered when I knocked politely. I am Freedom Ford of the *Herald Democrat*, or at least they let me string for them, and I know what brings you here to this den of iniquity, but don't you think you should put your pants on first?"

He asked, "Before I do what? You have the advantage on me this cold gray morn, Miss Freedom. I don't know what you're talking about!"

She said, "You are a famous federal lawman, up this way to investigate the crimes our corrupt City Marshal Duggan refuses to investigate, if indeed he is not party to them!"

Longarm started to say he was there for no such thing. Then he told her to wait in the lobby whilst he got dressed, adding, "We'll talk about it in the hotel restaurant downstairs as I wake myself up with some coffee."

She chortled, "Oh, goody, an exclusive!" and scampered off down the hall like one of the pupils she should have been pestering at such an ungodly hour.

Longarm considered the newspaper stringer's wild charges as he made himself presentable with a fresh shirt and underwear under the same tweed suit. He and the current city marshal of Leadville, Mart Duggan, went back a ways. Longarm had been there when two gunfighters had killed one another at the narrow guage stop and Duggan had added the both of them to his claimed score. Duggan was one of those assholes who really carved notches in his gun grips like a bad man in a Ned Buntline Western yarn. But after that you got what you paid for and Leadville could have hired worse.

The thuggish Mart Duggan had replaced their Marshal O'Conner who'd been shot by one of his own copper badges, Officer Bloodworth. Nobody knew why. Bloodworth had outridden the posse and never been caught.

Once installed as their new town law, the flashy Mart Duggan stunned everyone by enforing the law even Steven, with neither fear nor favor. Or else he just enjoyed running in rich or poor, broadcloth or denim, and even black or white.

The written city ordinances forbidding heathen Chinese on the streets of Leadville were of course enforced with casual brutality by Duggan and his jovial bully boys. Duggan wasn't about to give the big shots who'd appointed him the excuse to fire him just because he'd disappointed them.

And yet . . . that made *two* local voices suggesting that federal money might have been purloined by the Leadville P.D. and such things could happen and *had* happened out this way.

When he went downstairs he found Freedom Ford on her feet by the archway betwixt the lobby and the hotel restaurant. As he escorted her in she said she'd already had her own breakfast but mayhaps she could go for some marmalade on toast with her coffee.

As she stared in wonder at their table near the window, Longarm ordered a more substantial breakfast.

"You're not going to eat all that!" she decided as the waitress served them with a tolerant smile. She was more familiar with the eating habits of healthy working men. Albeit few ordered fried eggs on top of chili con carne over *waffles*.

"I had a rough night," Longarm confided, adding, "Worked up a good appetite with my honest overtime efforts."

She asked, "What were you up to, stoking a blast furnace?"

He smiled fondly and replied, "Wasn't quite that hot. But it was hot enough to work up an appetite. You said you had something to charge your local peace officers with, Miss Freedom?"

She nodded and asked, "What would you say if I told you they fired the notorious Grant Webber for pistol-whipping a slow but honest beer-garden waiter?"

Longarm soberly replied, "I'd say they should have fired him. Some old boys can handle authority, some can't."

She asked, "What would you say if I told you the notorious Grant Webber just bought out about the biggest pig and chicken operations in Lake County, cash on the barrelhead?"

Longarm decided. "I'd say he must have been putting a little aside each month in a little tin box. How come you keep calling him notorious, Miss Freedom? I've never heard of the bully boy."

She said, "Nobody had ever heard of him until he led that raid and got to bragging about it over his cups. To hear him crow, one would think he'd arrested Frank and Jesse and Billy the Kid, the loudmouthed thing!"

Longarm nodded knowingly and said, "Some old boys get carried away by a good arrest. Who did this notorious Grant Webber arrest, ma'am?"

She said, "Oh, you know, that bank robber they arrested up this way a month or so ago. Officer Grant Webber led the raid on that house of ill repute the outlaw had been hiding out in."

Chapter 7

Army first sergeants and local lawmen found their jobs easier when they were cut from the same rough cloth. The late Sheriff Bill Brady of Lincoln County had *been* a first sergeant in the Union Army. As far as anyone could say, Mart Duggan's qualifications for his position as City Marshal of Leadville had been seven notches on his gun. But he appeared that same jovial bully it was best not to mess with when Longarm dropped by his office later that morning to log in officially.

Duggan offered him a cigar and he was smiling as he said, "It's about time you showed up here. Understand you favored not one, not two, but *three* separate women with your company across a table before you let us know you were in town and all?"

Longarm smiled back and asked, "Didn't you know, seeing you were keeping tabs on me that close?"

Duggan chuckled fondly and replied, "Me boys lost tabs on you when you and the Powerful Patricia left the Magic Flute Wine Garden in the middle of the show. What did that reporting girl want with yourself this morning at your hotel?"

Longarm said, "That's one of the bones I have to pick

53

with you. I understand you recently fired the man in charge during the arrest of the late Abner Prentiss, Mart?"

Duggan looked pained and said, "Had to. Old Grant meant well, I'm sure, but you can't be pistol-whipping a waiter just because they hang a badge on you. Old Grant got his name in the papers a while ago and I fear it went to his head."

Longarm lit the medium-priced-but-not-bad cigar to give himself the time to choose his words before he said, "I heard your Grant Webber lead the bunch that rounded up Abner Prentiss."

Duggan shrugged and said, "Oh, that? Yeah, he did get written up for that one, too. But earlier this year he won a shoot-out with a wanted killer, working as a security officer for one of the mines up this way. Before he'd changed his name for business reasons he'd made quite a rep in other parts as a man killer, and to tell the truth we hadn't thought old Grant had it in him. Called the killer man-to-man, and beat him to the draw fair and square. Just goes to show you. But once he was a famous killer in his own right, old Grant seemed to pick fights just to watch lesser men crawl. Had to let him go before he wound up gunning some innocent bucko while wearing Leadville P.D. on his chest."

Longarm said, "You done right, then. I hear tell he's in the pigs-and-chickens trade these days."

The man who'd fired Webber nodded and said, "Has to do *something* for a living. I know what you're thinking. But he never."

Longarm just cocked a brow.

Duggan suggested, "Let's not shit around, Uncle Sam. Everybody up here knows what you're up here after. Grant Webber was never alone with that lonesome bank robber before they brought him to me. I questioned Prentiss personally about the money he rode off with. He told me how he spent it all on wine and whiskey and wild,

wild women. He was lying like a rug, of course. We were able to figure he spent about two grand on a wild old time before we caught up with him. But we tore apart Madame Three Tits's cribs and the hotel he'd spent a couple of nights in before he moved in with them whores. So the rest of the money's still out there, somewhere. But Grant Webber ain't got it."

Longarm blew a thoughtful smoke ring and asked, "He *inherited* all them pigs and chickens from a kindly old uncle?"

Duggan shook his head and said, "Blood money, staked on cards, and old Grant's never been lucky in love. That wanted killer I just told you about had a five-hundred-dollar bounty posted on him. So Grant was able to buy into a serious poker game at the Taj Mahal and we all know how Lady Luck feels about poker players with deep pockets. Ran his original stake up to five figures in a game they're still talking about. It was while he was celebrating with his newfound friends he took to pistol-whipping a waiter with his badge on. When I took the tin star back he laughed and said he was too rich to associate with the likes of me."

Longarm grimaced and observed, "They tell similar tales of the wild-ass drunk who discovered the Comstock Lode and followed his swelled-up head to perdition. Ain't the Taj Mahal one of those wine theaters? How come they let him win all that money there? Just last night I sat up near the stage with a lady and a carafe of Chablis and nobody at any of the other tables was dealing cards."

The lawman who knew the town better explained, "The Taj Mahal ain't one place. It's more like a state of mind, owned and operated by this Englishwoman who used to live in India. In addition to the wine theater you just mentioned, she runs a card house right next door and hires out high-priced rooms with no questions asked under the one roof the two establishments share, along with her Taj

Mahal livery. The three in a row taking up most of her block fronting on State a short way north of the opera house."

Longarm thought, nodded, and said, "Corral and a smithy takes up the rest of the frontage. Handy place to rein in a jaded mount and get your own face upstairs and off the street. You say you know the hotel Abner Prentiss stayed at before he moved in with Madame Three Tits?"

Duggan said, "I've only the word of a lying gaboon he stayed anywhere. He *said* he spent his first nights in town at the Tabor Hotel. He did not. They'd never registered him there and he couldn't describe any of the rooms upstairs, even when I . . . *shook* him a bit, just to be after helping him recover his memory."

Longarm agreed it sure seemed a poser. Knowing they'd been watching him that night, he was glad as hell he'd gone back to his hotel from the Carbonate Spa in the wee small hours. So how was he supposed to pussyfoot into that infernal Taj Mahal now, even though it did have one of those back doors he'd tinkered with the night before?

Knowing Mart Duggan was a fairly sharp lawman for all his fandango showing off, Longarm knew better than to inspire second thoughts about Grant Webber's run of luck at the Taj Mahal by asking where his damned old pig farm was. Freedom Ford would know and she'd asked him to talk with her some more, bless her nosey hide. So he thanked the Leadville law and mumbled something about newspaper morgues as they shook and parted friendly.

He knew they'd be keeping an eye on him until they decided he was as lost in the dark as they were. Duggan his fool self was likely drawing less than a thousand a year with his deputies lucky to take home five hundred, along with whatever they could collect in graft. Hence, it followed as the night follows the day that few if any of

56

the Leadville P.D. meant to share a dime of the loot with their federal government and at least some of them would be willing to kill for that kind of money.

Although one might never guess it from the glowing accounts of town tamers in the *Police Gazette*, in the case of the far-famed cowboy or Indian-fighting cavalry trooper, hard-riding men on the side of the law could be hired for little more than day-labor wages and *that*, Josephine, was why so many of them were ever eager to hit it rich by hook or by crook.

Walking along State in the sunshine, Longarm considered the odds of a bully with an uncontrollable temper winning the price of even a small spread at high-stakes poker. Then he considered the odds an outlaw on the run might check into a proper hotel, all cleaned up with his breath under control and no lathered pony out front, before he'd spent at least one night in a no-questions roost *above a wine theater* with a feed sack of incriminating evidence to hide, and decided. "Makes more sense that way. But let's not build any castles in the sky before we see if they have possible foundations."

Longarm hadn't asked Mart Duggan how they'd figured Abner Prentiss was holed up with Cherry Poppins in that other shady rest because it seemed obvious and he hadn't wanted to inspire speculations about wine theaters. The ruthless but romantic Prentiss hadn't seen that despite how innocent *he* might look, he and his substitute truelove had been turning heads everywhere they went in Leadville. They'd simply been trailed to her business address by one or more of Duggan's deputies, or "officers," as old Hod Tabor preferred to call his up-to-date police force. Had anyone else in town turned in Prentiss they'd have put in for the reward and . . . Now *that* was something to study on.

Unlike federal deputies, local lawmen were allowed and

encouraged to apply for federal bounty money. So who'd applied for the price on Abner Prentiss?

Longarm strode on down to the Western Union near the 6th and State post office to get off a progress report and ask some questions before he dropped by the *Herald Democrat* to ask about their Freedom Ford.

When they got done laughing, an older cuss wearing a green eyeshade and sleeve garters sniffed, "If you're talking about Scoop Ford, the famous female reporter, she don't put out to begin with, and after that she's just a stringer we pay space rates now and again when she brings in something worth running."

Another newspaper man volunteered, "That ain't often. The kid means well but she's inclined to report tall stories the hard-rockers tell her just for fun. What might you want with old Scoop, pilgrim?"

Longarm had been a green army recruit, a green cowhand, a lot of green things in his time, and there'd always been know-it-all assholes talking about *him* that way and he'd always hated it. So he drew himself up, flashed his badge and I.D. and said, "I ain't exactly a pilgrim. I am Deputy U.S. Marshal Custis Long of the Denver District Court and I have come to offer the exclusive I promised Miss Freedom Ford in exchange for a hot lead she gave me earlier."

A younger male reporter gasped. "No shit? Hell, I know twice as much as little Scoop about everything! Just ask me anything and I'll prove it!"

Longarm said, "Ain't got toad squat to ask *you*. I aim to talk to Freedom Ford. So where's she at?"

They told him. When she wasn't trying to be a newspaper stringer she sewed dresses in her cottage over on Alder Street, on the wrong side of the narrow gauge tracks, damn it to hell.

They were talking over a quarter of a mile and she was just a fool stringer. But he'd shot his mouth off and so he thanked them for their help and trudged east across town as the sun and the dust rose higher. The acrid fumes of the smelters surrounding the town on all sides never got better or worse.

Freedom Ford's frame cottage had been cut by the same cookie cutter as the others in that part of town. Their roofs were tar paper. Their siding was vertical board and baton, stained slate gray by the fumes and fly ash drifting on the vagrant mountain breezes. She'd planted marigolds along the drip line out front. The rest of her front yard, like those to either side, was bare grit. You had to dig some to find any soil in Leadville.

When the newspaper woman who'd pounded him awake that morning came to her own door in answer to his knocking she was wearing one of those blue smocks French artists or mayhaps seamstresses worked in. She sure looked surprised to see him. For a moment he expected her to tell him to go away. He'd have been willing. Then she invited him in and sat him down at a window seat near the sewing machine she'd been treading when he'd knocked.

She said she'd put the coffee on and assured him her marble cake was only a day or so from the bakery. Then, as she turned away from him to do right by a guest she suddenly swayed, grabbed hold her kitchen table, and tried to hold it in as her shoulders shook under her loose artist's smock. Longarm rose to join her, but stood behind her as he soberly observed, "When I first came west after the war I knew my way around a farm and the army had taught me how to shoot and salute. But I had a time learning to rope and throw. So they called me 'the Kid' and made fun of me 'til it was all I could do to keep from losing my temper the way they wanted me to. This one top hand liked to heat one side of a china plate over the camp fire, holding it by the cool side as he ladled out chili con carne to hand to me, innocently suggesting I watch out 'cause Mex food could be hot."

She sobbed. "I didn't think you meant it! I thought you were only trying to get rid of me this morning! I thought you were mocking me the way they mock me over in that press room."

He said, "You're newer at their game than they are. Nobody was ever born an old hand at anything. Everybody has to learn the ropes as they go along, and mocking the kid of the outfit never learns him one lick faster. I mentioned this in passing, a few years later, when I met up with that top hand I told you about. He was still drawing forty a month. He'd never made ramrod because nobody liked him. I'd sort of moved up in the world in the meantime, but for old times' sake I bet him a month's wages I could now rope and throw a calf faster than he could."

He let that sink in and said, "He was afraid to make the bet. A hand living month to month can't afford to bet that sort of dinero. So about that exclusive, if you want to work with me on this case . . ."

He was suddenly aware she wasn't wearing all that much under her blue artist's smock as he found her in his arms with her pert nose buried in his tweed vest, bawling fit to bust.

So, being a natural man, he hugged her closer, with one hand in the small of her back and one finger naturally fitting in the crack of her firm little ass.

Freedom Ford suddenly stiffened and warned, "Deputy Long, I don't know what they told you at the *Herald Democrat*, but I'm not that sort of a girl!"

He said he'd never though she was as he got a politer grip on her.

She sighed wearily and asked if he still wanted to work with her.

He said, "I do. I got questions about your town I don't

want to talk to anybody else about. The one hand washes the other, even when they both behave themselves. So stick with me and you might just wind up with a byline in the *Post* or *Rocky Mountain News.*"

She gasped, "Surely you jest! What kind of a story are we working on, Deputy Long?"

He said, "My friends call me Custis. I don't *know* what we're working on, yet. That's how come I could use some help."

Chapter 8

In fairness to the pressroom jokers who'd dismissed her as a green kid, once he had her calmed down enough to start serving him coffee, cake, and current events in Leadville, Longarm did find Freedom Ford inclined to swallow conspiracy notions without salt or soothing syrup.

Most everyone in Colorado knew Governor Fred Pitkin openly favored the mining and beef barons who'd backed his election and to hell with anybody in their way. It was no secret Silver Dollar Tabor was carrying on openly with the beautiful but dumb "Baby" Doe, née Lizzy McCourt, after just plain buying her from her hard-up husband, Harvey Doe, for a thousand in cash and those vice charges fixed by a judge Tabor drank with.

After that the not quite as beautiful Freedom Ford felt sure the Freemasons were out to take over the United States whilst the Elders of Zion were out to take over the whole world unless the Yellow Peril washing across the Pacific didn't swallow everybody first. She was as certain City Marshal Duggan and his hard-cased roundsmen were in for shares with Leadville's notorious "Legion of Footpads" said to roam the "next street over" in vicious wolf packs that could strip an unwary drunk down to his socks and run off, laughing, by the time he knew he might be in trouble.

As in all such mining camps across the late Victorian world from the Welsh collieries down to South Africa and west to Australia, prices were high and standards of decency were low. Newcomers lucky enough to afford anything until they could sign on anywhere flopped two to a bunk with total strangers under lice-infested blankets at four bits an eight-hour shift or slumped on the sawdust-covered floors of saloons if they'd bought two bits' worth of "cold medicine" first.

They called pneumonia a cold in Leadville, where the thin air above ten thousand feet was laced with rock flour, fly ash, soot, and smelter fumes. Desperate men ordered meals they couldn't pay for, hoping for a few nights in jail, but paying for their transgression with one hell of a beating, if they were lucky. The unclaimed bodies of dead cats or friendless bums just disappeared off the streets of Leadville. Some said they went into the ever-roaring smelter flames. Others said they went down the shafts of played-out mines, with other trash. Freedom Ford was dead certain that once you dried a corpse out it burned better than cordwood. She said she had it on good authority they fired up railroad locomotives and river steamers in Egypt Land with those mummy folk they kept digging up all the time.

The hell of it was, Longarm had heard the same thing. You just never knew about such gossip. Maybe the formidable Augusta Tabor *was* holed up in that $40,000 Denver mansion whilst her husband and his Baby Doe held court in Leadville's luxurious Claredon House. Mayhaps those markings that Italian astronomer had mapped on another planet *were* canals dug by somebody mighty unusual. Freedom Ford just served what she'd heard or read along with her pretty good coffee and sort of stale cake.

Longarm broke out his notebook to jot down the names while he was able to ask questions he wasn't ready to have anybody else in town all that aware he'd asked. She didn't seem to worry about separating the wheat from the chaffe and Longarm had learned the hard way how two witnesses could offer three versions of what they'd seen.

Freedom Ford said she hadn't been there but felt sure they could trust the words of those present who'd seen things her way. She said that now-legendary gunfight between the suddenly wealthy Grant Webber and the notorious Wig Gruber had looked more like premeditated murder to more than one honest mining man she knew.

Longarm asked her how to spell "Wig" and allowed he'd never heard that one.

She said, "I understand it was short for Ludwig. Wig Gruber was a Dutchman, like the owners of the Warmerbroder Mine he guarded against high-graders. They say his job was cut out for him because the lode was chrysolite, richer in silver than lead carbonate, and it seems to be true Wig had shot other high-graders up in the Montana goldfields."

He asked her to get on to the shoot-out, asking, "How come a *lawman* shot a private dick for . . . Oh, that's right. Wig Gruber had a price on his head, posted up Montana way. So then . . . ?"

She said she understood the shooting had taken place in the wine theater of that Taj Mahal conglomeration. A mining man she trusted had told her there hadn't been anything one might call a shoot-out. Grant Webber had been bellied to the bar when Wig Gruber came in for the supper show after his shift at the Warmerbroder. Nothing was said. The witness had Grant Webber simply turning around from the bar with his gun already out to fire point-blank without warning. Another witness had recalled Grant Webber saying, "Wig Gruber, I arrest you in the name of the law!" as the Dutchman lay staring at the ceiling at his feet, with five bullet holes you could have covered with one playing card smouldering up from his shirt.

Longarm shrugged and said, "I agree that wasn't sporting of Grant Webber. But that's the way it can go when a man has a dead-or-alive posted on his head. I understand the townsfolk of Northfield opened up on the James Younger gang first, as they were coming out of that bank. You have to expect others to shoot first and say their piece later when you have a rep for winning fair fights."

She pouted and said, "He was *paid* to murder that tough security man. I'm not talking about the five-hundred-dollar bounty. I'm talking about his sudden run of luck at cards, right next door to where he gunned down Wig Gruber like a dog!"

"Who do you reckon paid him, and for what?" Longarm asked mildly.

She said, "The high-graders. Thieves who'd been warned by Wig Gruber not ever to pause to light a smoke within pistol shot of the mine adit he and his crew were guarding for the twisted sisters."

"The twisted what?" he asked, and laughed.

She half rose from her seat across the table to top off his coffee as she explained, "Dutch pansies, swishy boys, queers, the two Dutch partners who own the Warmerbroder. A Dutch-speaking mining man I know says that's what Warmerbroder means in Dutch. They say Kurt Zukor gets to play the husband while fat Adolf Furstmann gets to be the wife. The two of them hired Wig Gruber to make the bigger boys leave them alone. They say poor little Adolf had a hissy fit when Grant Webber shot Wig."

"Do they say who's holding the high-graders at bay since then?" he asked.

He wrote down the name, Gus Steiner, when Freedom said the sissy partners had replaced a known killer with a husky Dutchman who said not to mess with him. Old

Henry down in Denver would have it on file if Gus Steiner was wanted anywhere for anything serious.

As he dunked some stale cake in his coffee, that helped some, Longarm asked her to explain that payoff she'd alleged.

She sat back down to flatly state, "A few days after he gunned down Wig Gruber, Grant Webber went head-to-head with Johnny Dart in a high-stakes game of draw poker they say went on around the clock. Grant Webber was never a big winner within human memory. Johnny Dart's a professional and, more important, a Cousin Jack, like most of the high-graders up this way, see?"

Longarm saw what she was getting at. He wasn't sure it was fair. You called a hard-rock mining man from Cornwall, England, a Cousin Jack as distinguished from a Welsh Taffy, an English Terrier, or an Irish Navvy, hiring them in that order of preference before you hired someone who couldn't speak English. The Cornish Cousin Jacks mantained with rough justice they'd invented hard-rock mining back when Bronze Age ships with painted sails had come all the way from the Holy Lands to barter for Cornish tin dug with deer antlers from granite shattered by charcoal flames and cold water. They'd been working to get better for many a year since, and since nobody could argue they weren't the best, they were accused of being the most talented high-graders.

High-grading was the dangerous but profitable selective theft of particular color. Any mining man who knew his muck, or loose ore ready to be transported to the smelters, could single out a four- or six-pound rock with a hundred times the metal content of the one right next to it. "Native" or pure nuggets of lead-silver alloy often fell away with no rock at all attached when you blew rich face-rock. In sum, a thief who knew his oats could stuff his pockets with a hundred or so dollars in high-grade within minutes, if you let him. So old boys were forever getting shot as they stepped behind some ore trams or around back of a stamping mill to "take a leak."

As to a high-rolling gambler of Cornish descent fronting for a gang of Cousin Jacks to pay off a lawman who'd rid them of a pest, it sure sounded complexicated.

Longarm asked, "Wouldn't it have been easier, and surely way more discreet, simply to leave the payoff where Grant Webber could find it? Why go to all the bother of deliberately throwing a poker game in front of God and everybody?"

She said, "You just answered that, Custis. How was an honest lawman drawing three figures a year supposed to account for all the money he was about to come into? The bounty on Wig Gruber wasn't going to be enough to buy the poultry-and-pork operation he meant to own free and clear. It's my understanding there were other financial considerations driving him. A poor but head-turning widow with bodacious debts and in need of a strong rich man to lean on. So they say between that bounty money and his sudden luck at draw poker, Grant Webber had close to a hundred thousand in the bank when Mart Duggan allowed him to resign."

Longarm said, "Duggan told me, just today, he *fired* Webber. But your way sounds more sinister. That's the trouble with favoring minor odds and ends that make for a better story. We all do it. Stories without any plot or point ain't as much fun. But that's the way real life tends to play out. In spite of that poem about moving fingers writing, there ain't nobody writing us a slick script we have to follow. We just up and *do* things. Most of them ain't been thought out before it's too late to be more clever. That's how come we always *say* we got off a good one at the teacher, the boss, the judge, whoever. I wish I had a nickel for all the clever parting shots I never said, or a chance to take back stubborn notions that cost me and those I never aimed to hurt, because nobody was writing me better lines!"

He saw he had her thinking. Before that led them off in another direction he asked her where Grant Webber was holed up with all his sudden wealth.

She said Grant Webber and his lady friend, that handsome young widow, were said to be shacked up on his new spread, an older spread he'd bought off the harder working Scandinavians who'd fenced and proven a quarter section of Mountain Park out by Turquoise Lake. So he thanked her, said he'd get back to her, and legged it back to the center of town where, hoping to kill two birds with one stone, he hired a cordovan mare and a center-fire stock saddle from the Taj Mahal livery.

Knowing his way around Leadville from earlier visits, he knew east-west 6th Street turned into the Turquoise Lake Road eight or ten blocks west. The lake itself was an aptly named expanse of snow-melt in the afternoon shade of the higher spine of the continental divide. The lake lay six or eight miles out. He'd ridden less than five when he came to the fifteen-feet-across "sunwheel" landmark, offered by Indians who'd been there earlier than the Ute, and who had laid it out across the grass, in skull-sized rocks. From there he could see the newly peeled spruce poles of the Webber spread's proud gate.

He heeled his livery mare on over, calling out, "Hello, the house!" as they rode in, braced for yard dogs.

Nobody barked. It was getting on toward supper time but no smoke was rising from the chimney, and from the way the pigs were squealing, now that they were closer, nobody had slopped them recently.

He repeated his call as he dismounted in the dooryard. There came no answer. He tethered the mare to the hitch rail and strode over to knock. He saw the front door was barely ajar, and sensed someone peeking out at him. He called, "I see you, too, and don't you think we ought to cut out this shit?"

Receiving no answer he drew his six-gun as he moved in and kicked hard. The door flew in as somebody screamed in the dark interior. It sounded like a kid. Long-arm tore on in and slid along the wall to get out of the light from the doorway as he declared, "It's all right! I'm the law! I come in peace!"

A sad scared voice sobbed, "I want my mamma!" and now he saw them, over in the far corner. A little gal of about six or seven was holding the three- or four-year-old who wanted his mamma. They were both barefoot in flour-sack shifts to suit either sex as badly. They were both in need of a bath. The little girl said, "Please don't hurt us, mister. We aint been bad!"

He soothed, "I can see that, sis. Where are your folk, and ain't it past your supper time?"

The little girl said, "I don't know where mamma and Uncle Grant went. We didn't have supper last night, neither. But I fed Sonny, here, some chicken feed and a couple of eggs I boiled, earlier. You're not fixing to hurt us, are you, mister?"

Chapter 9

It made no sense. But he soon established there were no responsible or irresponsible adults on the premises. So he put his gun away and had to care for the kids before the critters.

This didn't pan out, though, at first. The canned goods on hand had been literally too hard for a six-year-old. There didn't seem to be a single can opener, but Longarm had a can opening blade on his pocket knife, and there were plenty of pans, and a water pump out back. So he stoked the kitchen stove from the wood pile in the yard, got it lit, and fed the kids cold pork and beans whilst they waited for the bully beef and canned vegetable stew he'd whipped up to boil some. From the way they both dug in he could see the little girl's improvised meals of boiled eggs and chicken feed hadn't been enough to hold them.

But, as every cow camp cook knows, you could eat canned pork and beans cold without ill effect and he had some with them as they waited for the main course.

He'd already been introduced to Sonny. The little girl said her name was Daisy. Their mamma had been Edith Bordon before she'd met up with Uncle Grant Webber. From their cheerful names and good manners, Longarm decided he liked their mamma but couldn't tell Sonny where she was, even though he kept asking.

Once he'd served out their warm simple stew, Longarm left them at it whilst he looked after the critters.

The summer sun set early that close to the looming continental divide, but you could still see colors as he led the livery mare around to the back, unsaddled her, replaced her bridle with a rope halter hanging in the empty stable shed, and turned her loose in the fenced-in pasture, saying, "Have some grass and I'll be back to see about water. We're likely to be here a spell!"

In the henhouse he found more than half the chickens dead or dying. When leghorns had no water they stopped laying for a spell. Then they started dying. Longarm hauled a couple of buckets in for the low trough along one wall before he commenced to pitchfork the dead birds outside.

Once he had the survivors provided with feed and water he locked up and headed for the pig pens. There were eight pens in a row, with four mighty unhappy hogs to a pen. None had died yet, but half of 'em were down. Longarm filled their troughs before he slopped them with the cracked corn mash he whipped up, tossing the dead leghorns in to waste not and want not. It looked disgusting. But that was pigs for you.

Toting water to the empty trough near the pasture gate, Longarm told the mare when she came over, "Something bad has happened here, Brownie. Folk don't volunteer to ride off and leave their kids and livestock to thirst and starve. Both kids need a bath, but neither has lice. They were put to bed in them shifts by a caring mother. After that it gets scary!"

He went back inside. It was dark enough now for him to light the oil lamp haging above the table. The kids had cleaned their plates and wanted more. He said, "Your eyes are bigger than your stomachs. You've had enough for

71

now. Let it settle some and I might feed you a can of peaches off that top shelf."

Daisy started to cry.

He said, "Aw, for Pete's sake, you're likely to wind up with belly aches if I slop you like hogs after you've missed some meals."

She sniffed and said, "I ain't crying 'cause I'm hungry. I'm crying 'cause my mamma always says our eyes are bigger than our stomachs, and then she laughs, and we miss her and want her to come home, mister!"

Longarm suggested, "Call me Uncle Custis if you like. I miss your mamma, too. I can't leave you and Sonny here alone. So I reckon we'll just have to wait 'til she and your uncle Grant, or somebody, shows up to take care of you."

Sonny kept looking out the window, big-eyed. Daisy moved around to put an arm around him, confiding to Longarm, "He's afraid of the dark. I'm not afraid of the dark, most times. Last night I cried along with him, because we heard the haunts all around outside."

Longarm moved over to the cold fireplace and hunkered down to make things cozier as he chided, "Ain't no such things as haunts, Daisy."

She shook her uncombed head to reply, "That ain't so, Uncle Custis. Ain't you heard how grownups all got to die and then turn into haunts?"

Spreading juniper bark kindling on a crumpled sheet of newsprint from the corner pile Longarm said, "I've heard it. Don't believe it. Who's been telling you such things, Daisy?"

She answered, innocently, "Uncle Grant. He's scared of haunts when he's been sipping the medicine he takes for his old wounds. Uncle Grant was wounded in a war one time, and has to sip a lot of medicine before he can sleep at night."

Longarm started building the night fire atop the kindling as he told her, "Uncle Grant sounds like a swell gent. What else does he talk about when he's been at his medicine?"

She said, "Sometimes he fusses at Mamma. What's a 'fuckingslut,' Uncle Custis?"

Longarm struck a light to a corner of the crumpled newsprint as he told her, "A not-nice lady. But we know your mamma's nice, don't we? Sometimes when folk have had too much . . . medicine, they say things they don't mean. Your uncle Grant was just funning about haunts, too. Like I said, there ain't no haunts."

She gravely asked, "How do you know, Uncle Custis? How can you tell what just went bump in the dark when you can't *see* in the dark?"

Adjusting a sliver of kindling to burn brighter, Longarm told Daisy, "You *can't* always tell what's going bump in the dark. There would be no point in having light if we could see in the dark. But you can tell it wasn't a haunt because there'd be no point in *dying* if folk got up to pester others after they were *dead*. You can't get up to pester anybody when you're feeling poorly, or you've had too much of Uncle Grant's medicine. You can get a gent to just lay there if you give him a good lick upside the head. How's he supposed to get up and go after you've *killed* him?"

She said, "I don't know. Uncle Grant said he saw a man that was nothing but dry bones peeking in yonder window at us one night."

Longarm said, "Walking skeletons make less sense than animated corpses. If any critter could move its bare framework around without any muscles attached, Professor Darwin would have discovered at least a single specimen. There just ain't no such animal."

Sonny sniffed. "I'm scared! Where's our mamma?"

Daisy soothed. "She's coming back, Sonny. She's surely coming back."

Then she stared owl-eyed at Longarm to gasp, "Oh, no! What if something bad has happened and Mamma comes back to us as a *haunt*?"

Longarm rose as the night fire began to blaze and moved over to take the two kids back to the table, choosing his words as he began to see how religions got started. He said, "Set down and I'll open that can of peaches. I ain't saying there are such things. I still say there ain't. But the way I hear it, haunts come back to scare the ones who've done them wrong. Ain't that the way *you've* heard it?"

She nodded soberly and said, "Uncle Grant thinks a haunt named Wig is sore at him because they had a fight one time."

Reaching for the peaches, Longarm said, "There you go. You told me, earlier, how your mamma laughed when she fed you. So I'll bet she *liked* you, right?"

Daisy nodded and replied, "She told us she *loved* us and she'd see us in the morning when she tucked us in bed at night. Sometimes we'd hear her fussing at Uncle Grant but when I asked her about that she said to just remember she loved us no matter what."

Longarm said, "There you go. So even if your momma died and went to heaven and then came back to look you kids up again, she'd still be your mamma and she'd still love you, right?"

Daisy smiled timidly and said she guessed so.

Dishing out the canned peaches for the three of them, Longarm said, "You know so. Let's consider other likely haunts you might meet up with. Have you or Sonny, here, ever done dirty by anybody who ever died?"

She said, "We don't hardly know anybody who's died. Our real daddy died when Sonny was just born and I was little. I don't see why *he'd* be mad at us and we don't remember the old folk back East who must have died, I guess."

74

Longarm said, "There you go. All the dead folk you kids know betwixt you would be *friendly* haunts if there was any such thing as a haunt. Did you ever see this Wig Gruber haunting your uncle Grant?"

She gravely replied, "No. Mamma didn't see him, neither, and Mamma is a grownup."

Longarm sat down to sample his own peach dessert as he assured her she only had to worry about dead folk *she'd* done dirty.

It seemed to work.

By 9:00 the warm food and cozy fire had both kids calmed down to where he could talk them both into sponge baths, a change of flour sack smocks, and a short bedtime story before they let him tuck them in bed up in the sleeping loft.

Daisy said her mamma and uncle Grant had stayed down below after the lights were out, sometimes fussing and sometimes making funnier noises.

Longarm climbed down to recline atop the covers of the sleeping pallet he found in a corner under the loft as he lit a cheroot and asked it, "Now where do you reckon the motherfucker hid her body? He must have killed her. She'd have never stayed away this long if she could manage to crawl home to her kids, knowing they were alone here!"

As the night fire he'd lit died down to glowing embers, Longarm told those faces forming in the gathering darkness to go away and leave him be. As a lawman he knew the danger of picturing faces you'd never seen. He knew that however the real Edith and Grant Webber looked in real life, they wouldn't look like the sweet-faced matron and weak-chinned mean drunk he kept picturing.

Folk you'd never seen never looked the way you pictured them. Even as he tried not to picture the missing couple, Frank, Jessie, Black Bart, and Billy the Kid were walking past other lawmen with their bare faces hanging

75

out, unrecognized by their hunters, who'd formed different mental images of them.

Blowing smoke out both nostrils like a pissed-off bull, Logarm marveled, "I'm playing button button, who's got the button, with no more notion what I'm doing than those two kids up above me have of what in blue blazes is going on!

"Did Grant Webber buy this place with the money I've been sent out to find? Did he buy it with blood money from other crooks entire? Did he really win that fucking card game? None of them answers works any better than the others. All them answers raise more questions that are just as tough to eliminate and now I can't even *ask* the fucker where he got the money!"

Next morning he got up the kids, fed them, and rummaged through drawers until he found regular duds, shoes, and socks for them to put on. Then he gave them some chores to keep them busy while he rode up the wagon trace to where Daisy said "Aunt Alice," a friend of her mamma, lived with "Uncle Walt."

Their name was Hendersen. They were Swedes, but all right, with kids of their own. They hadn't known anything was wrong at a neighbor spread seven furlongs away. When Longarm told them what he'd found they said they'd be proud to take Daisy and Sonny in and suggested their own two eldest boys could as easily check the Webber stock twice a day as drive it up their way. Walt Hendersen and his whole family followed Longarm back on their buckboard to pick up the abandoned kids. From the way little Sonny whooped when he saw the younger Hendersen kids, Longarm figured it was going to work, for now.

As his wife and older kids were loading Daisy, Sonny, and some of their personal belongings aboard, Walt Hendersen had a quick look about with Longarm, complimented him on his earlier tidy-up, and decided, "I reckon we can hold the fort for neighbor Webber 'til you find out what happened. Ain't much stock, it's all penned good, and . . . That's funny, but I see Grant's already cut and cured his hay. Saves us the bother . . . I reckon."

Longarm followed his gaze to the distant hay stack in the freshly mowed fallow forty and asked, "What am I missing? I wasn't riz in this high country. Don't you usually commence haying this late in your summer?"

The homesteader shook his head and said, "Summers start later at that altitude. So that grass was still a tad green to cut and dry. But since anyone can see Grant *done* it. He must have thought he knew what he was doing."

A big gray cat got up and turned around three times in Longarm's gut.

Leaving his livery mare tethered near the buckboard, he started out across the fallow forty on foot. Walt Hendersen followed. As one of his kids started to tag along the agreeable Swede said, "Lars, go steady our team for your mother. Don't let none of the other kids follow us."

Young Lars did as he was told with no argument. Walt Hendersen was that sort of father. He didn't ask what they were doing. He hoped he was wrong.

Longarm was hoping so, too. Then the wind shifted as they got closer to the haystack. You could smell right off the newly mowed hay hadn't been cured before someone had stacked it a ways from the house, likely late at night. The damp heat of fermentation had hastened the formation of more ominous odors as well. Both men knew what they were smelling before they got there. They'd both ridden in the war and once you smelled that smell you never mistook it for anything else.

Longarm only had to haul out an armful or so near the bottom before he'd exposed a woman's high-button shoes, with feet still in them. He swore and hunkered down. Walt Hendersen hunkered beside him. Each man took one ankle and together they pulled. The dead woman's soggy dress wound up around her tits by the time they'd hauled her out on the stubble of the mowed field. Longarm wasn't surprised when Walt Hendersen gasped, "Oh, dear Lord, it's Miss Edith! Do you think Grant Webber did this to her?"

"I doubt she committed suicide," a stone-faced Longarm replied.

Chapter 10

It only felt like it was taking forever. Things went way
smoother than Longarm could have hoped to manage
alone. Walt told Alice enough in Swedish to send her and
their buckboard streaking as her man and their eldest boy,
Lars, stayed with Longarm to secure the scene of the
crime.

Lars had already showed he took orders from his elders
well. Longarm gave him detailed instructions and sent
him in to Leadville aboard the livery mare, at a lope.

As they watched the cordovan lope with such a light
load Longarm asked how come Walt and Alice hadn't
taught their kids to speak any Swedish.

Hendersen said, "Who would they speak it with and
sometimes there are things a man might want to say to
his wife that are none of their business!"

Longarm had given Lars the correct protocol. He'd
been told to stop at the Lake County sheriff's department
near 6th and State before he rode on to alert Freedom
Ford. But the anxious newspaper gal beat the county riders back with Lars by better than a quarter hour.

She rode in sidesaddle on another hired nag, this one a

retired army bay gelding with a few miles left in its twelve-year-old limbs.

The army remount officers sold off mounts at the age of eight, no matter what shape they might be. in, and that was why you saw so many livery nags branded U.S. Long-arm waved her down in the dooryard and helped her dismount as he warned, "What I have to show you ain't a pretty sight, Miss Freedom. But I promised you some scoops, so, are you up to a dead body that's . . . been dead a spell?"

She gulped and replied, "I don't know. The few I've ever seen have been fairly fresh. Who's body are we talking about?"

He told her all he knew before they were close enough to smell Edith Webber because he didn't know that much. Once they'd laid the dead woman out on the stubble he'd hauled her skirts down to cover more of her mottled flesh. He'd figured the county coroner wouldn't have wanted him to wipe the straw chaffe out of her blankly staring dove-gray eyes. He'd wished one could. The young mother's eyes were the same color as her daughter, Daisy's.

Freedom made it within conversational distance of the corpse before she dug in her heels and gasped, "Give me time to get used to this. I don't want to throw up if it can be avoided! Lars, here, said it was her own husband who . . . did that, and wasn't she in a family way when he did it to her?"

Longarm steadied her with an arm around her shoulder as he told her, "I can only make educated guesses until they autopsy her over in the county seat. Her neck would be as mottled and swollen in any case. It's as likely he used the proverbial blunt instrument. They'll find blood in her brain case if he killed her *that* way. Since we never rolled her over, she might have been shot in the back. That's why they perform autopsies. She might have been expecting. On the other hand, men and women both bloat even more than that for the first few days. Let's hope he only took one life, here."

Freedom was gamely taking shorthand notes as she swallowed hard and asked, "What happens after they bloat all they want to?"

He said, "I doubt anybody wants to. Sometimes they bust their seams. Then the bloating goes down as they dry more and start to turn black. Left to its druthers where plenty of air can circulate, a dead body sort of slowly but surely cremates down to what looks like soot mixed with sun-bleached bones. All sorts of really funny stuff goes on when you throw in sealed coffins, attempts at embalming, and so forth. This forensic gal I know allows she finds the chemistry fascinating. I'd as soon let them who enjoy such fascination worry about it."

Freedom gasped, "My God! She's alive! She just winked her eyelid!"

Longarm said, "No, she never. The eggs the blowflies laid in her open eyes are commencing to hatch."

Freedom fought free to run around to the other side of the haystack and throw up. Longarm didn't follow. He'd thrown up before she'd ever gotten there.

To their credit as members of the human race, the four Lake County deputies who rode in just as Freedom was about recovered looked about as upset at the sight of the murdered young mother. Though, being they were county riders and the fool reporter taking notes was a *gal*, they tried not to let their feelings show.

Longarm had explained to Freedom before their arrival why the city marshal she suspected of everything but whooping cough had no jurisdiction this far outside the Leadville city limits. So she didn't ask that dumb question and you could see her confidence grow as she mostly kept her mouth shut, her ears open, and her pencil jotting.

Walt Hendersen wound up doing most of the talking.

81

Being a neighbor he could tell the other riders way more than Longarm could about folk he'd never met in life. He had to admit to his chagrin he still had no idea what the murderous Grant Webber looked like.

Hendersen described his missing neighbor as medium height and regular featured save a gold front tooth and bushy black brows. Said Webber had acted decent enough, sober. Hendersen had never seen him drunk. It was his wife, Alice, who'd said that the dead lady at their feet had been worried about his drinking after sundown. It appeared Webber was afraid of the dark for some reason and needed that medicine for his nerves.

As the investigation droned on and commenced to repeat itself, Longarm took Freedom inside and brewed them some coffee. As she sat at the pine table she asked him why lawmen went over the same points again and again.

He said, "It's something like looking for the keys you know you left somewheres around the house. You got to keep looking in the same places 'til you look in the right one, or, in this case, give up in a while. It's doubtful we'll find anything else out here. But it ain't right to quit before you've tried sincere."

As he poked up the coals in the kitchen stove Longarm added, "They expect me to stick around and ride back to town with them. You ain't a witness. You're free to leave anytime. So if I were you I'd get back to your *Herald Democrat* with all that shorthand before they might be offered your story by somebody else."

She jumped to her feet, demanding, "Who else in this world *has* my scoop? It's mine alone!"

He shrugged and said, "It seems to be, so far. Some of those county men may want to make sure the *Herald Democrat* spells their names right."

She stood tiptoe to give him a quick peck on the cheek, then she lit out like an alley cat with turpentine under its tail and Longarm got to drink all the first pot he made. He figured the others would be ready for the next pot by the time he brewed one at an unhurried pace.

He was right. Their coffee was just commencing to get cold when they stamped in to ask him what he was doing, decided that had surely been thoughtful of him, and gathered round the table to get down to brass tacks.

They'd agreed it was certain the late Edith Webber had been done in by a person or persons unknown, with her common-law husband the most likely suspect. Neighbor Hendersen had described the son of a bitch and the two horses the Webbers had kept out back, a paint and a gray, seen at some distance. It seemed obvious that having killed his woman in a drunken rage, the known man-killer had dragged her out in the fallow forty, run the horse-drawn mower late at night when nobody was watching, and piled all that uncured hay on her body before riding off on one horse, leading the other, with some serious riding in mind.

So they'd sent Walt Hendersen home to his own woman but asked young Lars to carry another message into town, confirming there was really a customer for the county coroner out by the lake.

It took another forever and the whole blamed day was going on shot by the time they all rode back to town with Miss Edith under a tarp in the one-horse morgue ambulance.

Back in town, Longarm felt he *ought* to go around to the tailgate of the ambulance and assure Miss Edith her kids were being looked after. He knew it would look dumb and figured she already knew if there was anything to the Good Book, whilst there'd be no sense talking to her if there wasn't.

So he rode on back to the Taj Mahal livery to dismount out front and hand the reins over to a colored stable boy, who promised to be right back with his security money.

83

He was standing there lighting a smoke when he suddenly seemed tangled up with a whole lot of perfumed calico going, "Oh, thank you, thank you, thank you!"

It seemed only natural to laugh and kiss such a happy little gal. So he did, and she didn't kiss back like such a little gal.

As they came up for air Longarm asked, "Might this mean they mean to run your story in the *Herald Democrat*?"

She said, "Oh, are they ever, with a byline, and they've put it out on the wires for me, demanding space rates and a byline all across this land, and you *are* going to tell me first as soon as you catch that poor woman's killer, aren't you?"

To which he could only reply, "It depends, Miss Freedom. I might or might not have due cause to make a federal arrest. I don't have a lick of jurisdiction if murder-most-foul is all I can prove him guilty of."

The stable boy came back with his security. Longarm tipped him a dime and sent him back inside grinning. Freedom pouted, and said, "What could be worse than murder-most-foul? Didn't you see what that brute *did* to that poor woman?"

Longarm glanced up at the sun. It was low in the sky again and those mountains to the west tended to end cloudless afternoons the way you pinched out candle wicks. Waving up at the white plaster arabesque facade of the next-door wine theater, Longarm suggested they talk about it inside, where he could mayhaps kill two birds with one stone.

She said she'd never been in such a place before. But like the old maid who kissed the clock, she was willing to try anything, once.

It was barely going on early supper time. So the orchestra pit was still empty and they had no trouble getting a table smack against its brass rail. When a waitress with a British accent despite her harem-gal outfit came to take their orders, Longarm ordered a magnum of red burgundy to last them and asked if they could get anything to eat at their table.

She said the Taj Mahal grille wasn't serving yet, but allowed she might be able to rustle them up some Welsh rabbit. He said that sounded swell. When they were alone again Freedom repeated her question about murder-most-foul.

Longarm said, "It ain't nice, it's true, but it ain't a federal offense. It's up to the local district attorney to convince the state of Colorado it ought to hang somebody for the murder of Edith Webber. I was sent up here with the power to arrest any sneak holding a whole lot of Uncle Sam's money."

He was able to bring her up to speed on his mission by the time the harem girl came back with their generous helpings of Welsh rabbit.

Freedom fooled with her entrée dubiously, tasted, and decided she was hungrier than she'd thought. But as she dug in she asked, "Why do you call this Welsh rabbit? It appears to be grilled cheese and toast if you ask me!"

He said, "That's about what it is. Calling it Welsh rabbit is a joke, like Swiss steak, mock turtle, French coffee. That cheese is *pretending* it's more expensive rabbit meat, see?"

She said, "Tastes all right to me. How come they call it a *Welsh* rabbit?"

He shrugged and said, "The folk here are English. If they were Welsh they'd likely call it English rabbit."

He didn't know her well enough, yet, to mention what Greek pals had told him about *Greeks* calling boy-buggering the "English vice," or that the French called the French pox the "Spanish disease." He contented himself with observing, "It's human nature to put down other breeds. Don't it beat all how that nationalistic Know

85

Nothing party want to keep all this country for real Americans who were here first, now that they've taken it away from the American Indians who were here first?"

She repeated her gossip about Grant Webber assassinating Dutchmen for English, or at least Cornish highgraders.

He said, "That's why I want to treat you to a bite to eat and at least the first show here. I'm out to establish myself as just another sucker. Later on, should anyone wonder aloud who I might be or what I might want, I'm hoping someone else will say I was in here earlier with some gal who seems to have got away."

She asked, "Why do you want me to get away? I can help you sneak all about better if I stick around. What if somebody caught us off somewheres and we were holding hands and spooning instead of looking like a lawman and an investigative reporter?"

He suggested they play it by ear for now and not make any moves before they sat through the early show.

She agreed but asked what they were looking for in this Taj Mahal conglomerate.

He said, "If I knew I wouldn't need to look. This place has a shady rep and it's established that quantities of money have been exchanged on these premises by shady characters. If Webber came by his sudden fortune as a paid assassin, it ain't my call; if he recovered money hidden upstairs in the no-questions-asked section it is."

She said, "I see what you mean! This is all so thrilling! How are we ever going to pussyfoot around up yonder where you naughty boys and wicked women meet for sneaky-sneaky?"

It was a good question.

He decided to wait until they'd both had more wine before he made the obvious suggestion.

Chapter 11

Freedom Ford was too inclined to jump to conclusions, but she asked intelligent questions. As a small inexpensive band filed in, dressed as posh Limey butlers, she made Longarm go over possible connections between the bank-robbing Abner Prentiss, the fired lawman Grant Webber, and the hot-sheets rooms to let upstairs.

He said, "There may not be any. A few first nights Prentiss spent up this way before he settled down with Cherry Poppins ain't been accounted for and he *said* he'd hidden the bulk of his ill-gotten gains above a wine theater, which this is."

"Unless he hid it in that house of ill repute," she demured.

Longarm said, "If he was lying to me at the foot of the gallows all bets are off and I may as well start searching for the money in the real Taj Mahal in India or that Leaning Tower of Pisa. Having said that, if he'd hidden the money on the premises where he was arrested, it would hardly be hidden this evening. The lawmen who raided the place knew he'd left Camp Weld with fifty grand and after *they* searched in vain for the loot, the ladies who do business there have had the time to probe top to bottom with their hat pins and magnifying glasses."

He poured more wine for her as he added, "We know Grant Webber had a lot more than the town council ever paid him before they fired him. We can safely assume he never found it where they arrested Prentiss. Either one or both of them could have put in some time above us in what I have heard described as a rabbit's warren of hidey-holes for hire."

As the musicians began to tune their instruments Freedom grimaced and raised her voice to say, "I understand why an outlaw might go to high ground like a fox up a tree, but what about Grant Webber? He was a lawman 'til they fired him. What might he have been doing up yonder, paying outrageous nightly rates?"

Longarm dryly observed, "I understand some rooms rent by the hour if you bring your own . . . bedding. In all fairness, Webber might have prowled about upstairs for the same reasons lawmen prowl similar hidey-holes across this land of opportunity. You've no idea the arrests we make in no-questions-asked surroundings. Riders of the Owlhoot Trail exchange such addresses, and a man blowing into a strange town with a price on his head and night coming on swirls into such murky backwaters the way trash floating down the Big Muddy might."

The musicians began to play the "William Tell Overture," badly. So she had to speak louder as she asked, "Why didn't Grant Webber arrest that young bank robber here at the Taj Mahal, then?"

Longarm shook his head and said, "If he had, we wouldn't be jawing about *other* places. It's possible that once he took part in the arrest, Webber recognized the prisoner as someone he'd seen staying here, earlier. In which case Abner Prentiss would have mounted that gallows without ever knowing his cache had been uncovered."

He took a sip of wine, sighed, and added, "It's just as

likely I've run canals betwixt dim blotches on a distant planet, and Webber was paid off by high-graders, as you suggested, for killing a tough Dutchman."

He let that sink in before he said, "*Or,* if you *really* want to mount a swamping conspiracy, what if a Leadville lawman with a mean streak recognized a mine security man as a wanted outlaw, gunned him dirty but lawfully, and ran his honestly obtained reward money up into the sky, playing draw poker next door, just like he said?"

She said, "Pooh. That's no scoop worth running on any front page. How do you mean to learn if things could possibly be that simple?"

It was a good question and the stuffy-looking bass fiddle player was giving them dirty looks. So he suggested they shut up and take in the show for now. He knew that from the other tables farther from the stage his pretty table-mate was inspiring others to look him over as well. That was why they were seated so close to the orchestra pit.

Regulars never gave a second thought to other regulars they might run in to going or coming from the crapper, or mayhaps turned around down a wrong hall.

By now most of the other tables were occupied, mostly by men in pairs or quartets. Some sort of fuss had started over in a far corner as the musicians struck up another atmospheric oriental tune. In this case the one about Peggy Gordon. Then the curtain went up and everybody clapped hands for the snake-charming gal with Irish features and this serious-looking python wrapped around her bared middle.

Their Oriental waitress came by to clear away their dishes and ask if they needed anything else.

Longarm said they were fine but asked what that fuss at the other table had been about. The Lime Juice gal in harem duds glanced down at the cheese-smeared dishes on her tray to sniff. "Welsh rabbit. How was I to know

Taffies want us to call it Welsh *rare*bit, the great silly sods? I assured them had I been out to insult Welshmen I'd have told the one about kittens baked in a pie!"

Longarm soothed, "Some like to split hairs. You get many orders for Scottish and soda from your customers?"

She laughed weakly and said, "I had one the other night who objected to Scottish. He said he was Albanian."

Longarm said, "I suspect *Albanach* was the term he used. Some Scottish folk in Denver told me Scotch, Scots, and Scottish are all *English* words for *Albanach* if you wanted to get *picky*."

She said she didn't care and carried the dirty dishes back to the grill next door. Freedom Ford asked what that had all been about. He said, "Human nature. Spanish-speaking folk act just as picky about how you pronounce their words for blue or prairie, with each side looking down on the other."

He pointed his chin at the snake dancer up on the stage, who mostly stood there whilst her python did all the wig-wagging, and added, "I read somewhere about some Hindu called a Thugee, who allowed it was *him* agin' his brothers, his *brothers* and him agin' their *cousins*, his brothers and his cousins and him against the *rest* of his caste, and so on out to everybody in India against the confounded English Raj. Like I said, human nature."

Freedom Ford giggled, threw her head back, and recited:

"Pity the plight of the Hindoo,
He does the best he kin do.
  He sticks to his caste
  From first to last,
And for pants he makes his skin do."

He said, "Go easy on that burgundy, it's stronger than beer and the night is young."

She said, "Pooh. I'm not feeling drunk. I'm feeling liberated. My mamma told me, just before I left home to seek my fortune as a woman who knew shorthand, she'd named me Freedom in the hopes I'd never be stuck in the flypaper before I'd flown some. My dad didn't like the notion much, but as she was helping me pack, my mamma grabbed hold of me all of a sudden and made me promise I wouldn't marry up with the first man who asked. I'm not sure why she said that. I know she married up at sixteen but she seemed to get along all right with my dad."

He looked away and said, "Grass is always greener and the institution has its advantages, if you want to live in an institution. We were talking about the English-speaking caste system. You told me there's a lot of that going round up here in Leadville?"

She sipped more wine and said, "English- and Dutch-speaking. Silver Dollar Tabor's faction and the Dutch faction led by his rival mining baron, August Rische."

Longarm replied, "Do tell? I thought August Rische and Hod Tabor were former business partners and good pals. Didn't they both go from nothing much to having it all just a few summers back when storekeeper Tabor grubstaked a Dutch prospector to a few dollars' worth of grub and a gallon of white lightning?"

She owlishly replied, "Rische and his partner, George Hook, struck it so rich they could never forgive Hod Tabor. They owed him a one-third interest in their Little Pittsburgh and he'd known them when it was agreed August Rische was too poor to feed his yellow dog."

She sipped more wine, ignoring his warning look, and continued, "Hook eventually sold out and went home to Germany. August Rische got a quarter million for his share in the Little Pittsburgh and stayed on here to get richer grubstaking other prospectors, mostly fellow Dutchmen. How come we have so many Dutchmen, Irishmen, and Chinamen in this land of ours of late, Custis?"

He said, "The Irish and Chinese can't find work where

they grew up. A heap of Dutchmen have left home to avoid the higher taxes and wilder notions of that Prussian kaiser and Mr. Bismarck. We were talking about a feud betwixt our resident mining magnates?"

She said, "They say August Rische is fit to be tied, having found the first silver our Silver Dollar Tabor crows so loud about. Starting out with no more than his shares in the Little Pittsburgh, Hod Tabor—or, in point of fact, his thrifty wife, Miss Augusta—went on to own or hold shares in ever richer mines, along with his opera house, saloons, sawmills, and such, including that bank with real brick walls. They say he sleeps in a two-hundred-dollar nightshirt with a mistress he bought from her husband for a thousand. Being a Scotsman, Hod Tabor likes to march down State Street sporting a feathered highland bonnet, a Royal Stuart kilt, and a silver mounted broadsword at the head of his bagpipe band on any and all public occasions—and leave us not forget his *wife's* name is *Augusta*!"

Longarm frowned thoughtfully.

The somewhat sloshed local gal asked, "Don't you get it? All the time Hod Tabor's been screwing his Augusta he's been screwing August Rische!"

Longarm started to say that sounded crazy. But he'd read about this head doctor over to Vienna town who said folk could act more loco over shitty little imagined insults than an honest punch in the nose. So he asked her to tell him more about the bitterness betwixt the English- and Dutch-speaking denizens of Leadville.

Freedom said that as his being elected mayor might indicate, Silver Dollar Tabor still swung the most weight aroung Lake County. But as that Welsh miner at that other table had just demonstrated, the English-speaking mish-mash hailing from all parts of the British Empire, Canada, and these United States were only agreed that furreners who didn't speak their common lingo were worse than any infernal Limies, Harps, Jocks, Taffies, Cousin Jacks, Damn Yankees, or Johnny Rebs.

The Sauerkrauts, as she described them, presented a smaller but more united front. It was widely held that Dutchmen could be dangerous as well as too damned stubborn to abide.

He said, "Great. I didn't have *enough* red herrings I have to eliminate. You just handed me another possible motive for all that gun play within easy earshot of this very table!"

Freedom Ford said, *"Wheee!"* and lowered her head to the table across from him as the curtain came down and the lights went up.

It wasn't clear whether the crowd assembled was applauding the snake dancer or the pretty little thing with her brown hair coming unbound across that orchestra-row table. Longarm reached across to shake her gently as he murmured, "Aw, don't pass out on me, Miss Freedom!"

She mumbled something that sounded a lot like, "Oh, go fuck yourself."

So he let her be and leaned back as if he'd come in with somebody else.

That same waitress came back to lean over and whisper, "Clientele are not allowed to sleep on the tables, sir."

He said, "She ain't asleep. She's had too much to drink and I'll bet you a dollar you'll be understanding enough to let her just rest there a spell."

The waitress shook her head and said, "They're holding the curtain for the next act and I have orders to tidy up this table. Do you have more like *ten* dollars to spend on your sleeping beauty?"

When he allowed he might she said, "Then pick her up and follow me."

So he did. Freedom was a small gal and didn't struggle in his arms as they followed the harem gal cum waitress through the jeering crowd and up a flight of stairs taking them above the lamplight of the main floor where someone was whooping, "Powder River and bang her once for me, cowboy!"

The invisible waitress ahead of them opened a door in the blackness to reveal a much brighter albeit still dimly lit corridor as she confided to Longarm, "I hope you understand this isn't a hotel and we are only, ah, providing private accommodations where an indisposed patron or more might recover."

He followed her into the small but dramatic "accommodation," fixed up the way everyone but Orientals pictured an Oriental oda, as you called a harem chamber set aside for fornication.

The English gal dressed as a harem gal waited until Longarm spread the more modestly dressed American gal across the four-poster fitted out with enough pillows for a bunkhouse before she told him, "That will be ten dollars, please, and we don't really want to know when the two of you may choose to check out. Just leave the door ajar so the towel girls will be able to see it's safe to enter."

Longarm handed her the ten dollars with an extra silver cartwheel and her tone was suddenly warmer as she said, "Enjoy yourselves and we hope you'll come again."

Then she'd left, giggling, and Longarm was free to giggle some himself, until he considered how the pretty little thing sprawled helpless there was likely to react when, not if, she came to in a harem oda with him or any other natural man.

Out in the darker corridor a more regal woman of a certain age had stopped the waitress to ask who they had in crib seventeen. The younger waitress said, "More quality than usual, Miss Binnie. Well-dressed stockman in town for the sights if I read his hat and boots right. Not too drunk, polite enough, considering, and I suspect the lady he wants to be alone with may still live at home. A little country, with no signs of a recently removed wedding band on her lightly suntanned hands. Trust me, Miss Binnie. I look all of them over good, before I bring them up here."

Miss Binnie Bodmin, American citizen born in India of Cornish stock further back than she cared to admit, said, "Keep an eye on them and don't hire out anymore cribs just now, Joy. We've just gotten word the law is looking for that Grant Webber who used to stay up here with his partner's wife. So we're liable to have unwelcome visitors and I do so find it tiresome to pay out extra protection money!"

Chapter 12

As every man who's done much hunting or fishing knows, once you get into position to do some still-hunting or pole-fishing it's best just to keep still and let the critters get used to you. There's a murmur in the air where danger ain't, out of human ken a ways. Citified folk who don't know this are inclined to comment on how *quiet* it is out in the country. They don't know a moving human, like a prowling wolf, moves about in its own big blob of silence.

Country folk, red or white, like the country critters around them, can hear serious matters pussyfooting through the woods because they seldom make any noise. And neither do most of the critters keeping a wary eye on them.

Crows and jay birds fuss at bears and barefoot boys. But the crickets stop chirping, the squirrels stop chasing one another through the trees, the lizards, mice, and other skittersome leaf rustlers just freeze in fear and, just like the city folk say, it gets quiet as hell in the country.

Having learned as a barefoot boy to sit quiet in the dappled shade a few minutes longer than he felt like it before the leaves all around got to rustling and anything from deer mice to deer might come back out to play,

Longarm sensed the dead silence all around could mean he and his sleeping beauty, yonder, were still inspiring others to listen.

He lit a cheroot as he sat on the rug with his back braced against the bed and quietly murmured to the unconscious Freedom Ford, "Got to give the mice and cockroaches time to forget we're up here. Got to do some serious reconsidering of the original plan as well."

She murmured, "We'd best say good night, Jimmy. This isn't fair to either of us."

He said, "Knowing I'm being tailed around town by Duggan's copper badges, and if I'm lucky that's *all* I have to worry about, calls for a new deal with a fresh deck. Billy Vail would never forgive me if I got shot for a cat burglar and Duggan's tails are *good*. I never knew 'til he told me they'd been tallying every gal I talked to in their town!"

Freedom protested, "Stop that, Jimmy! You know I want to, but my dad's a light sleeper and . . . Not here on this fool porch swing, you silly!"

Longarm decided, "There has to be a better way. Even if I had one of them cloaks of invisibility, there's just too much space above the wine theaters of this infernal town for one man to cover, groping blind. We got to figure out how to eliminate most of it. Narrow the search to where Abner Prentiss *was*, not where he *might* have been when he hid that money!"

Having the privacy as well as the time where he was, Longarm rolled some of the oriental carpeting he was sitting on out of the way. When he saw the flooring, which keeping with the oriental decor of the Taj Mahal was for Gawd's sake arabesque tiles made in Mexico and set in grout, he muttered, "This can't be the place."

As a self-taught man inclined to read most anything, Longarm knew you laid tile flooring in frame buildings over plywood, waterproofed and left tacky for the tiles with Stockholm tar. The late bank-robbing Abner Prentiss would have had a time prying up floorboards in crib seventeen!

Blowing a thoughtful smoke ring, Longarm decided, "If the other cribs for rent have tile floors like this one, we can eliminate 'em. We don't need to look under every carpet in every crib. If more than a couple or so are decorated the same as this one, Abner pried up those floorboards somewheres else!"

He hadn't said that loudly. Freedom Ford still sat bolt upright to demand, "Where am I? How did I get . . . ? Oh, my God, I'm in *bed* and you're still here and . . . We *didn't*, did we, Custis?"

He smiled wistfully and assured her, "Not hardly. I'd have surely taken my hat off. You're upstairs at the Taj Mahal. You tricked them into hiring us a room upstairs by pretending to pass out downstairs. Don't you remember?"

She said, "Dear Lord, was I that drunk? That red wine didn't taste that strong and . . . You say we've rented a . . . place of assignation over a wine theater? How much are they charging us?"

He said, "A week's salary or a month's rent for most working stiffs in this land of opportunity. I reckon somebody saw an opportunity to help hard-rockers spend their higher pay."

She laughed weakly and mused, "I wonder if they'll pay me space rates for my confessions of a white slave. Make a better story if I passed out smoking opium, though. So, anyway, I was sipping cider through a straw when this heathen Chinee, or make that a Hindu—"

He asked, "Why fake newspaper stories when the real deal promises to read better? How do you like 'Daring Girl Reporter Helps Recover Missing Federal Funds'?"

She swung her high buttons around to perch on the side

98

of the bed beside him as she chortled, "Goody! What do you want me to do first?"

He said, "Rustle leaves. Nobody out in the hall is likely to wonder why it's so quiet in here if it ain't so quiet. I want to pussyfoot around up here. Might be a whole lot easier if it kept sounding like we were both still in here. You reckon you could manage that?"

"You mean, talk to myself like an old maid gone off her rocker?" she asked with an incredulous smile.

He said, "Not hardly. Don't want anyone passing by outside all that interested. What if you got out your notes? I carried your bag up with you and it's yonder on the lamp table. What if you got out your notes and sort of went through them like you were editing them, mentioning out loud anything you liked or didn't like. Would't that pass, through a closed door, for the casual sounds of . . . well, pillow talk?"

She blushed and called him a dirty thing before she laughed and said she'd do it.

They gave it a try. Longarm rose to stand by the door as Freedom got a few pages into her shorthand to softly murmur, "Let's see now, the west winds off Turquise Lake failed to sweep the sickly sweet scent of death from the Webber pasture as—"

"Too preachy. Sounds like your reading me a bedtime story and I fear that might strike some as . . . unlikely."

She nodded and murmured in an even softer tone, "Check spelling for Turquois. . . . Adjective first or last . . . ? Pasture . . . Going on late in the afternoon . . . Never drank coffee . . . What the hell does this mean? Oh, sure, 'DY' for Daisy. . . ."

He said, "Better. Space your mumbles out more. Fall silent whilst you count say thirty to ninety under your breath."

He had her sounding good as he cracked the door to peer out into the dimly lit corridor. He listened tight.

Someone a few doors down was cutting up. Sounded like some cuss singing to a gal with a shrill and dirty laugh. Nobody else seemed to care. He ticked his hat brim at the gal on the bed and slipped outside to shut their door behind him.

As he passed the noisier couple the cuss was bellowing:

> "Came there a knock upon me doorstep,
> Who should it be but One Ball Riley,
> Two horse pistols in his hands,
> Looking for the man who shagged his
>   daughter!"

Another door suddenly popped open to catch Longarm flatfooted with his bare face hanging out as the other man in an undershirt and nothing else yelled, "Will you for Chrissake knock it off, you asshole?"

As their eyes met, Longarm said, "It wasn't me! Listen! You can still hear the asshole!"

The burly gent in the undershirt said, "That's for sure! Just wait 'til I get my pants on! I'll show him!"

Longarm soothed, "Hold on. He's stopped. Our message must have gotten through to him. Reckon I'll go back to . . . bed."

The other man grinned like a dirty dog and allowed he was suddenly feeling sleepy, too. They both laughed. The other man shut his door and Longarm muttered, "If that don't mean just three cribs occupied up here, nobody else gives a shit!"

Taking the bull by the horns, Longarm grabbed the next doorknob he came to and yanked it open to step inside and shut it before he struck a match. He found himself in an oda much like the one in which Freedom was reading her shorthand aloud. It only took a moment to establish the floor was tile under the Belgian Moorish rug.

Two more empty cribs told the same story. He tried a

door on the other side of the corridor, once more stepping into the darkness and shutting the door before he struck a light.

It looked as if he were in somebody's root cellar, up under a high mansard roof. Jars and jars filled the shelves all around and the smell was nigh overpowering in a delicious way. He moved over to hold the flickering match near what looked like mason jars nobody had put tops to. He picked up a jar, sniffed, and marveled, "Ginger beer, way in the Colorado sky!"

He found the floorboards of the storeroom more interesting. He liked ginger beer as well as the next cuss on a hot summer day and somebody hereabouts was making the real thing, not the watered-down shit they sold at the fair grounds. The Lime Juicers had learned about ginger beer in India, where the fermenting sugar and spices feeding a Hindu yeast had the alcohol content of ale. They'd told him a widow woman from British India owned the Taj Mahal.

The floor of her storeroom, ginger brewery, or whatever, consisted of one-inch lumber nailed to the joists. He hunkered down to hold the match light close. He saw no evidence any of the nail heads had been tampered with since they'd been driven home and allowed to rust some. This far back they weren't over the wine theater downstairs, either. He figured they were over the dressing rooms behind the stage. Letting it go for now he straightened up and shook out the match.

He was about to open the door when he heard somebody coming. It got worse. He flattened against the wall to be behind the door as it opened inward to spill candlelight across the floorboards he'd just been looking at!

A harem gal he didn't know stepped past him with the candlestick in one hand to reach for a jar of ginger beer with the other. She paused to sniff thoughtfully, dismissed the smell of matches with a shrug, and turned to step past

101

Longarm and plunge him back into utter darkness as she shut the door after herself.

Longarm held his breath as her footsteps faded away and somewhere in the night another door slammed shut. Then he inhaled all the thin air of Leadville he could manage and it still didn't feel like enough.

He forced himself to count a hundred Mississippis under his breath and then, since a lot of old snipers knew that trick, he counted a hundred more before he cracked the door open.

The hall was once more empty. He moved along it on the balls of his feet. As he passed where that cuss had been singing he heard the same woman laughing. He'd thought that was her carrying on until he got to crib seventeen to pause with his hand on the knob and a thoughtful frown on his face. For that sure didn't sound like anybody reading shorthand notes in there.

"Oh, yes, yes, don't take it out! Don't ever take it out, my great big huggy bear!" sobbed a familiar voice.

It sure sounded as if somebody had joined the party since last he'd been in crib seventeen. But if she were getting raped she didn't seem to mind it!

"Oh, no, not in *there*, Custis! You're too big for me to take it in my poo-poo!"

Longarm figured it was safe to assume that since he was out in the hall she couldn't be addressing him in yonder. So he twisted the knob to slip inside, shut the door after him, and turn to blink down at the fully dressed gal writhing around on the covers, rolling her head from side to side and begging him to be gentle until she looked up to see the expression on his face.

Freedom smiled up sweetly and asked, "Was that convincing enough?"

He said, "It surely was. Who were you convincing just now?"

She said, "I've no idea. It sounded like a woman's foot-steps. She paused right outside, as if she was listening. I somehow didn't think a woman would think another woman reading shorthand notes was making love. So I . . . improvised."

He said, "I suspect we were both given a good scare by the same hired gal. She's long gone, with a jar of ginger beer."

"A jar of what?" she said, and blinked.

He said, "A sort of Hindu jungle mold that turns ground ginger root and brown sugar to ginger-beer fixings. The way other molds turn sour milk into cheese or cider into vinegar. They mean to strain it, and dilute it with lemon juices and such before they serve it. Let's not worry about it. Suffice to say she didn't spot me and you sure seem to know more about country matters than you let on, no offense."

She sat up, flustered, and confessed, "I meant what I said when I said I'm not that kind of girl. But I never told you I was a blushing schoolgirl, did I?"

Longarm took off his hat and jacket before he hung his gun over a bedpost, dryly observing, "I'm sorry if you feel I've misjudged you. I meant no harm."

She sighed and said, "Well, I'm almost blushing. There haven't been that many. You see, when I was leaving home my mamma made me promise I wouldn't marry the first man who asked and a girl has feelings once she's already . . . had feelings, so . . ."

So a few minutes later, out in the hall, the widow Bodmin whispered to her male companion, "Fran must have imagined she smelled one of those waterproof Mexican matches in the storeroom. All three of our couples seem out to get their full ten dollars' worth of jolly old time."

Her bouncer whispered, "One of the customers down-stairs told me the one in this crib might be a lawman, like that Grant Webber who used to bring that married gal up here!"

Binnie Bodmin smiled wistfully and replied, "Lawmen have feelings, too, and listen to those bedsprings scream for mercy!"

Chapter 13

When he got her home after midnight, Longarm couldn't have gotten it up again with a block and tackle. But the wicked stage had lost a great actress when Freedom Ford had chosen a career in journalism instead. As he helped her down from their hired hansom she insisted he come in for a demitasse and they sent the driver on his way. Once inside she left the window blinds up for the old biddy she said lived across the way and lit her parlor lamp to shine on her male visitor as he doffed his hat but kept his jacket on whilst she brewed the coffee.

Sitting there fully dressed at a proper distance with her hands folded primly in her lap, Freedom demurely remarked, "If I didn't know she was watching I'd suck you off all the way this time!"

He chuckled fondly and said, "That would be nice, Miss Freedom, but mayhaps we ought to save some for next time."

She said, "I want you to suck both my titties in turn as I bounce up and down on top of you. But we're going to have to be discreet if we're to fuck more than two or three times a week. I have my reputation as a journalist to consider. I wouldn't want it known you gave me an exclusive just because I gave in to you!"

He soberly assured her, "I gave you your exclusive before you'd informed my how you'd been used and abused by every white man in Ohio and a couple of Indians since. What happened tonight at the Taj Mahal was the icing on the cake. We make a good team, in or out of the feathers."

She said, "I'll get you for that, dog style, but I'm serious about wanting to be discreet."

He said they'd likely work better together if they were. He didn't want to spook her, so he kept his idle speculations about Mart Duggan's copper badges watching them along with her neighbors whilst they sipped from her dainty French coffee cups, and then he got to his feet so they could shake hands in view of her front windows before she let him out with his hat in his hand.

As he put it on, striding away as she stood in her doorway, the lace curtains in the cottage across the way moved closer together as if in disappointment.

It was a hell of a walk to 4th and State after the beating he'd had to take from a really hard-up respectable seamstress cum journalist, now that she'd had her byline on the front page. But all things must pass if you just keep picking them up and laying them down. He didn't give a shit if anyone was tailing him. The long walk through the wee small hours would serve the fucker right.

As he limped through the lobby the night clerk told him there was a message in his box. He thanked the older man and took it upstairs with him. It only felt as if it weighed thirty pounds or so.

Up in his room, he lit the oil lamp above the washstand before he opened the envelope of lilac-scented ivory paper.

It was from the Powerful Patricia, she wanted to know where the hell he'd been that evening, though she worded it politer. He shot himself a sheepish grin in the mirror and said, "I know. But I didn't want the shy little virgin to think I was a sissy."

Then he treated himself to a whore bath with a damp rag while he softly sang:

> "Some folk say I am a knave,
> Some folk say I can't behave,
> Fucked a virgin to her grave,
> With my old orgran grinder!"

Then for some reason he was sound asleep before he'd made up his mind what he was going to say to the Powerful Patricia the next time he saw her.

A guilty conscience in the thin polluted air of Leadville sure could inspire interesting dreams. Playing bare-ass tag in a hay field with the petite brown-haired Freedom and the milky-skinned and black-haired Powerful Patricia would have been more fun if poor Edith Webber hadn't been standing there so still, just as bare assed but looking so damned dead. He could have gone downstairs and kissed the mule skinner who woke him from that dream with shouted suggestions to be very disrespectful to someone's mother.

After an early breakfast of steak and home fries with a side order of chili, Longarm went back to the Taj Mahal livery and hired a bay gelding for some casual riding closer to town. He didn't ask directions because he'd have told Mart Duggan where he was headed if he'd wanted company, overt or covert.

He'd located the Warmerbroder Mine on his survey map before leaving his hotel room. It lay out along the Mosquito Pass wagon trace running east betwixt the higher formations of Fryer and Carbonate Hills. It was said to produce richer chrysolite ore, which in the opinion of the Know Nothings, was more than any damned Dutchmen deserved.

As in the case of the unsung Cousin Jacks, Dutchmen played a greater part in the mining of the West than one might think from reading the lurid, local color books whipped up by hacks who neither knew nor cared to know Cornishman from other Anglos, nor High Dutch speakers from the patchwork "Germanic empire" Herr Bismarck was hammering together at the moment. But like Cousin Jack, Hans and Fritz had been hard-rock mining since before the dawn of history.

The comical costumes worn by gnomes in children's illustrated fairy tales were patterned after the leather outfits worn by hard-rock miners who'd provided the copper mixed with Cornish tin farther south to add up to the Bronze Age. The earliest scientific instruction books explaining how it was done had been written by a Dutchman named Agricola because he'd written it in church Latin even though his real name had been Georg Bauer, which meant farmer.

Since then in spite of being low-rated or laughed at by English-speaking mining men, Dutchmen had elbowed their way in pretty good all over the American West and some of them were tough enough to hold their own.

When the troopers at Fort Huachuca, deep in Apacheria, had warned a Dutch-American, Ed Schieffelin, he'd find nothing but his tombstone in the untamed Durango Mountains the stubborn Dutchman had said, "Fuck the Apache!" and set out alone with a seven-dollar mule to find and claim the famous Tombstone Lode.

A more mysterious Dutchman named Jake Walzer had started out as mining engineer for others and was now said to work a secret gold mine in the Tonto-infested Superstition Mountains east of Phoenix. Walzer literally fucked Apaches in the person of a nubile squaw, and would-be claim jumpers had a habit of disappearing in the Superstitions without comment in the part of Jake Walzer or his in-laws.

If the crusty hard-drinking Pancake Comstock was now famous as the prospector whose claims had given birth to Virginia City, it was only because he'd jumped the earlier claims of the star-crossed Grosch boys, Pennsylvania Dutchmen Lady Luck had just hated. For they had first recognized the complex chemistry of what was to become the Comstock Lode. But first the dispatch rider running their claim to Carson City had been murdered and robbed by road agents before Hosea Grosch gashed his foot with a pick and died slow but sure of lockjaw.

Then Ethan Grosch had borrowed money to bury his brother from good old Pancake Comstock and managed to freeze himself to death in the High Sierra, leaving Comstock the owner of the claim he'd be fucked out of in turn.

After a whole lot of cave-ins, another Dutchman, Philip Deisesheimer from Frieburg, had designed the timbering used in every hard-rock mine since. And then a sheer genius from Aachen named Adolf Sutro started crushing and refining ore before he drained the whole Comstock Lode with his twenty-five-thousand-foot Sutro Tunnel draining 1,277,500,000 gallons of mine seepage a year!

There in Leadville the rivalry betwixt the English-speaking faction led by Silver Dollar Tabor and the Dutch-speaking August Rische was none of Longarm's beeswax if all they wanted to do was kill one another. The long-standing feud simply had to be eliminated as the source of the missing Grant Webber's sudden wealth. If the Cousin Jacks had paid him to assassinate a square head before he'd murdered his wife, then bless his heart and the county was welcome to his neck.

Longarm knew if he failed to prove true those rumors about the shoot-out in the Taj Mahal, Webber had come by the money some other way and he'd just have to track down the murderous bastard!

The Warmerboder claim lay just north of the wagon

trace with the denuded and eroded slopes of Fryer's Hill rising in the near distance behind the complex of sun-silvered structures and rock-flour tailing piles in four-foot-high windows. As he rode in, a lean hungry figure in black, trimmed with German silver, stepped out of an office shed near the adit to softly remark with a slight accent, "That is far enough. Here we are not hiring. Here we coffee and cake no grub-line riders. *Sprechen Sie Deutsch?*"

Longarm said, "*Nein.* I'm the law. That's officious. You can play like a regular human being and I might be out of here in no time. So how do you want to play this tune? It's your call."

The yard dog decided, "If you're not a grub-line rider or pestering us for a job, come on in and we'll talk about it in the office. I'd be Gus Steiner. Forget anything you might have heard about my working for a pair of sissies. Mr. Furstmann is back East, consulting with an engineer named Lunkenheimer about draining his eternally flooding drifts. Mr. Zukor breathlessly awaits his return to their grand new mansion in Denver. *I* run things up *here!*"

As Longarm dismounted to lead the livery bay the rest of the way across the sharp gravel afoot he spotted more seriously armed pickets casually posted near the handy cover of higher tailings dumps, the solidly built stamping mill, and the high ground above the twin-tunnel adit. He felt no call to comment. Gus Steiner was either one of those straw bosses who couldn't delegate authority or he was on the prod.

Inside the deceptively flimsy office-shed with its frame walls in fact lined with sand bags and the hitch rail around in back so's even visiting horse flesh could be tethered out of the line of fire, Gus Steiner sat Longarm near his rolltop desk, produced a bottle filed under R for Rye, and poured two dangerous-looking drinks as Longarm explained, "I know it was before your time, but I'm interested in the gent you replaced, the late Ludwig Gruber."

Steiner, one of those odd-but-peculiarly-Dutch-looking men darker than most Italians, with bushy black brows and blue jowels that always seemed in need of a shave, handed his guest his drink as he bitched, "It wasn't before my time. I was his second in command and he was murdered by the law!"

Sitting down by his rolltop, Steiner explained, Wig was no outlaw. He was a security man with a job to do. The sticky-fingered high-grader they indicted him for killing in Montana was a rich kid vacationing out West for the summer. How was Wig supposed to know his Yankee daddy was in with that fucking Jew, Meyer Guggenheim? Never gun a friend of the Guggenheims in Montana. Montana courts don't care to hear a shit-for-brains kid had a gunny of high-grade in one fist and a Starr forty-five in the other when you did what you had to do!"

Longarm sipped his drink, it tasted more like brandy than rye, and replied, "What's done is done and Grant Webber got no more than five hundred for gunning down Gruber. What I'm interested in was all the extra funds he used to wind up in no time at all with a new family and a thriving poultry-and-pork operation close to a hungry well-paid market. I've established how, before he came into sudden wealth, old Grant was spending a good part of his city salary on high living along State Street. Your turn."

The swarthy Dutchman snorted, "Are you suggesting Webber collected an extra bonus for gunning Wig? Who do you suspect?"

Longarm said, "I'm working on motives. Off the top of the deck, one could start with his being a hard-cased Dutchman, no offense, in minefields dominated by a hard-cased English-speaking clique of drinking buddies. Your pal was gunned in a Hindu-looking establishment owned and operated by what I understand to be a lady born in

111

India to at least one Cornish parent. A heap of her customers are Cousin Jacks and I understand mining men of other persuasions suspect some Cornish plot to carry off all the loose ore in these parts."

Gus Steiner shrugged and said, "You hear rumors about some Cornish mastermind you can sell your high-grade to. He's said to own a played-out claim he still uses to explain the modest but steady tonnage of a mighty odd vein he says he's still following."

"How so odd?" asked Longarm before he took another sip.

Steiner said, "I'm a hired eye, not a mineralogist, but doesn't it seem odd to you a mine could produce carbonate, chloride, chrysolite, and even gold porphyry, which I understand you find *above* silver ore as a rule?"

Longarm whistled and asked if this mysterious mine had a name.

Steiner refilled his glass for him as he said, "Funny you should ask. I've been trying like hell to find a place to unload my stolen high-grade. Nobody can tell me where that Chinese opium den is where all those beautiful young white girls can be fucked so cheap, and I fear I am no longer interested in maps leading to the Seven Cities of Gold. It's just as possible Wig was done in by the fucking federation."

Longarm groaned, "Aw, shit, I hope we ain't talking about that new Western Federation of Mine Workers!"

Gus Steiner asked, "Why not? It's true Wig Gruber winged more than one trespasser on this property and scared the liver and lights out of even more. But he *really* liked to kick the shit out of organizers for the WFMW!"

He waved his own glass expansively and added, "Ask any of our boys if they want a fucking union and they'll tell you the same thing. We pay them three times what a cowboy makes and as we speak the cavalry is fighting bloodthirsty Apache for thirteen dollars a *month*! We have teenaged muckers down in the drifts making as much in three shifts and do you hear cowboys or cavalrymen bellyaching about needing any fucking union? It's all the fault of the fucking Jew, Karl Marx! No amount of wages is going to satisfy a working stiff once he reads how all working stiffs are being shit on by the boss no matter what the boss does. Wig Grubber warned Zukor and Furstmann not even to meet with those troublemakers from the WFMW not long before he was murdered by the law in the Taj Mahal."

Chapter 14

Longarm stared morosely down at the drink in his hand, even though he knew why it suddenly looked like a can of worms. He said, "I ought to thank you for pointing out yet another lead, or red herring, but I had enough on my plate already and, to tell the truth, I don't *want* to find out Wig Gruber was assassinated on orders from *anybody!*"

Steiner asked how come.

Longarm said, "Murder alone ain't a federal crime. They never sent me up this way to solve any pissy murders. I was sent to recover loot belonging to the federal government. If Grant Webber got all that money for gunning a Dutchman with a talent for making enemies, he *ain't the bird I'm looking for*, dad blast his eyes!"

Steiner nodded sagely and said, "It works better for you if Grant Webber just shot a wanted man because he was a lawman and stole that government payroll because he simply wanted it?"

Longarm nodded and growled, "Damned A. If he never recovered what I'm really after, Lake County is welcome to his neck and all you cranky mining men up this way are free to shoot each other or marry up with each other's sisters for all I care!"

He laughed at the picture and added, "Wouldn't it be a bitch if, just like the Know Nothings worry, the average white American turned out to be an Anglo-Dutch-Irish breed?"

Gus Steiner said he found the notion of his sister marrying up with a Cousin Jack or Irish union agitator too disgusting to contemplate.

Longarm said, "*Bueno*, we know the WFMW plays rough and has the money to back its play. Let's sniff about that mysterious mine producing ores of every color. To deliver his variegated rock to any of the legitimate smelters our mysterious mastermind would have to convince them he owned a mine. To own a mine you need a claim on file. So what sort of a claim am I looking for at the hall of records?"

Gus Steiner said, "Modest steady producer. Worked by a small crew, if not some crazy hermit alone. I'd look for an abandoned try hole or a worked-out claim refiled on by an optimist. Everyone up this way has heard the sad story of Jim Dexter's Robert E. Lee."

Longarm asked him to repeat it.

The local mining man said, "Poor Dexter had sunk fifteen thousand dollars and months of work into the Robert E. Lee without producing an ounce of silver. He was so discouraged that when he was offered enough to break even he climbed out of the ground without bothering to set off the last charges he'd drilled in."

Longarm brightened and said, "Oh, I remember hearing about that!"

Steiner said, "Everybody west of the Missouri did. The morning they took possession of the Robert E. Lee, the new owners set off the charges planted by the disgusted Jim Dexter with results heard round the West. They mucked silver-lead worth a hundred-and-twenty-five-thousand dollars from that first blast and made five-hundred-thousand dollars by the time they's spent sixty dollars in operating costs!"

Longarm sighed and said, "Remind me to buy me a coyote hole sometime when I'm a little ahead. Did you hear the opposite story about the empty hole in the ground salted with stolen high-grade and sold to a sap?"

Steiner shrugged and said, "That's what makes the game so interesting. How about the time Chicken Bill Lovell salted a bottomed-out try hole, sold it to Silver Dollar Tabor, and drank the money away, laughing, while Tabor in his ignorance told his men to keep digging eight feet deeper, into another hundred-thousand dollars a month for the dumb-lucky son of a bitch!"

Longarm didn't say it, but he suspected the surly Steiner, working for day wages to guard the holding of richer men, had struck close to the nerve of a maddening toothache.

Cowboys and cavalrymen didn't feel as put-upon as mining men making more because they were bossed around by human beings, men only eight or ten social cuts above them. Wages the mining magnates considered fair seemed insulting to men sweating twelve hours for three dollars when the boss wore two-hundred-dollar night shirts and talked million-dollar deals in front of the help. Longarm had never dug a dime's worth of ore for Silver Dollar Tabor and it still seemed unfair when he thought how a shopkeeper who'd never dug a ditch or even turned over a rock on his own could have wound up so rich shuffling silver stock certificates!

After politely turning down a third shot of rye, Longarm rode back to town, with more questions now than he'd started out to answer that morning.

After he'd returned the livery bay and dropped by the Western Union, he found a message from Freedom Ford waiting at his hotel and carried it into the hotel restaurant to scan as he had a one o'clock dinner.

By the time the bemused waitress brough his blue-plate special with a side order of chicken enchilada he'd sniffed on his way to the table, he'd read Freedom's follow-up on the Webber children and felt better about rich folk.

The formidable Augusta Tabor, not her flashy two-timing husband, had read Freedom's account of their mother's murder and wired imperious instructions that the tykes were to be taken under her wing down in Denver. While she'd been at it, she'd had Lake County seize Grant Webber's land from a felon and grant title to the kids he'd orphaned. When Miss Augusta yelled froggy around Leadville, everybody still jumped.

Longarm found her a good old gal in spite of what her husband's pals said about her being a tough old bag. He'd met her in the flesh and whilst she couldn't hold a candle to her young rival, Baby Doe, as far as form and figure went, old Augusta was smarter by half and a whole lot nicer than the Lincolnesque small-timer she'd made a multimillionaire out of. Miners who'd known them when had told Longarm how the big-mouthed Scot skinflint had only made out as a merchant in Slabtown because his Miss Augusta had been an "angel of mercy" to sick mining men and their dependents, slipping free candy to their kids, and extending credit to those down on their luck whilst her husband played cards with the ones in the money and, some said, cheated them.

"You mark my words, Hod Tabor," Longarm warned the sheets of paper in his hand. "You and your Baby Doe ain't likely to have a friend between you once your money runs out."

He set the notes aside and dug into his supper as he assured it, "Money runs out when you ain't making it anymore, and Miss Augusta was the one who said to grub-stake all those prospectors in these here hills whilst your Baby Doe was learning to spell c-a-t!"

The waitress, around thirty and close to beautiful had she lost say thirty pounds, came over to ask what he wanted.

Not wanting to sound like a sheep herder alone with his flock too long, Longarm told the buxom redhead in a white apron over calico he was wondering what they had for dessert.

She smiled down at his double order and said, "I'll fetch you the menu. Do I have time before you devour that light snack?"

He smiled up sheepishly and said, "Missed a couple of meals on my way up from Denver and they've been working me hard ever since."

The waitress dryly replied, "So I understand. She was very attractive."

That was what women called other women they were jealous of, "attractive." He idly wondered what she'd call the Powerful Patricia. He wondered harder how he was going to keep that big brunette and the little brunette from finding one another attractive.

As he moved Freedom's message aside to bring his enchiladas closer he noticed a bitty arrow on the last page. That often meant you were supposed to turn the page over.

He did and laughed with relief. For on the back of her last page Freedom had warned him not to call on her at her place until further notice because her sudden fame had all sorts of visitors coming to her door with all sorts of propositions, now that she'd gotten to be such a famous journalist.

The waitress asked what was so funny as she placed the menu on the table, moving the cut-glass bud vase with its spray of local blue-eyed grass to do so.

He said, "I was wondering what my plans for this evening might be. I was just now able to make up my mind for certain."

She said, "Sorry, I came on at noon, don't get off until midnight, and by then I'm just too tired, if you were that Prince of Wales and he were better looking!"

He laughed and said, "Just my luck. I find the girl of my dreams and she's in love with the Prince of Wales!"

They both laughed. He liked her spunk and it felt comfortable to flirt with good old gals who weren't ever going to take you up on it. He wasn't going to get to screw the Powerful Patricia until after midnight, most likely, and he made a mental note to picture that plump redhead sliding her own bare ass betwixt the sheets about the same time. It might have shocked her and disappointed him had he asked her if she wore a nightgown to bed.

He settled on plain old American apple pie, as Dutch as American beer, and her name turned out to be Lilo Feldmann, in spite of her red hair.

The Lake County Hall of Records was an easy walk from his hotel. But once there an elderly gent of the Hebrew persuasion explained why they couldn't help him much.

Mining claims were federal, filed with the Bureau of Land Managment, with the state and county in on the deal for tax purposes. So the county could give him a mighty long list of mining property holdings, but the county man doubted even the mining commission in Denver would be able to tell him in detail what the ore content of a given mine's day-to-day production might be.

The older man explained, "It's common to dig through gold-bearing gold pophyry into carbonates, chlorides, chrysolites and, around Leadville, a peculiar mishmash of iron, lead, and silver, in that order of percentage. They think it might have had something to do with the awesome events that split the buckled-up sea bottom of the Front Ranges from the buckled-up sea bottom of the higher continental divide to the west with all this bumpy lower ground in the middle. Acid water that can chew your boots off still bubbles out of the rock, the last places you want it, as you drill into what looks like solid rock of unlikely colors. A million years ago when we were all little red ducks, a hellfire chemical brew boiled up from the bowels of the earth through the birth pangs of these Rocky Mountains, and as it cooled and set, it set as veins of oxides, carbides, chlorides, sulfides, and God-knows-ides. Down at the Colorado School of Mines they show how you can dissolve metals in different acids and alkalies, pour test tubes on a pile of mixed clay, sand, and gravel and let it set as all sorts of pretty convincing ore. Mine claims are generally staked as gold, silver, copper, or whatever mines, but nobody *holds* you to it. Working a vein through gold to silver to copper, lead, or zinc is only to be expected. A lot of Arizona copper mines produce more nearly worthless uranium than the copper Mister Bell and Mister Edison need to wire up our world. A lot of California gold mines produce even more tungsten, speaking of by-product you can hardly give away. As I follow your line of inquiry, Deputy Long, you'll want a small owner-operated one-adit mine with its own arras-tra."

Longarm frowned and replied, "Arrastra? You mean one of those dug-in circles of stone you crush ore in by dragging a big rock round and round over it?"

The county man nodded and asked, "How else would you account for a chunk of this and a dab of that from different formations? They'd have to haul their stolen high-grade in the form of grit ground for the smelter chutes. They don't have geologists with chemical engineering diplomas reducing stamped ore to forty-pound ingots of lead silver to be shipped. The smelter hands are used to all sorts of odd ore. But they'd wonder if they saw a lump of white pophyry and black carbonate on the same shovel blade."

Longarm thanked him for the tip and said, "I got one more question and it's sort of delicate. I'd like it understood I have friends of your faith down in Denver. . . ."

"Some of *my* best friends are Jews." The older man nodded wearly and added, "*Nu*, what's the question?"

Longarm said, "The gossip has these rumor of high-grading inspired in part by the rivalry betwixt the English-speaking and Dutch-speaking mining men in these parts. I was wondering if you could tell me how serious it really is, from . . . your perspective."

The older man laughed dryly and said, "It could be worse. I could be shot on sight as a Chinese or, God forbid, an Indian. But both sides assure me some of their best friends are Jews, and what can I tell you? I just work here. Mining magnates named Bickle, Busch, Deidesheimer, Moshheimer, Neumann, Reis, Schussler, and so forth are welcome as the weeds of spring to your kind, and the Cousin Jacks resent everybody. But I don't buy into the clannish Cornishmen hiring paid assassins. It's never been their style. They prefer to outsmart men with Anglo-Scots names while looking down on everyone else with wry pity. I think that Ludwig Gruber simply got what was coming to him. They say he had a nasty temper."

Longarm said the county man had been a big help. They shook hands and parted friendly. There were seven smelters encircling Leadville. So Longarm hired another livery nag for some riding.

He had to start somewhere, so he rode out along Chestnut to work counterclockwise, and this turned out to have been a good move. At the third smelter he tried, after he'd explained to the foreman what he wanted, above the muffled roar of the compressed-air-fed flames, the burly, bearded Welshman called out, "Pen Gower! Come over here and talk to this lawman, look you! He may have the

121

answer to the strange muck we've been reducing for that coyote hole in California Gulch, you see!"

As they were joined by a younger Taffy, Longarm asked if it wasn't true California Gulch was said to be about played out and if they had any claims still left there to go with his suspicions.

The assistant said, "I do indeed. It was just the other day old Lyn Eddy delivered a dray of the odd muck. He says his Truro Mine has acid water running over alkaline chloride salts to bubble like the cauldron of a witch. But it's a rich brew, look you. High-grade indeed, yielding better than a thousand dollars a ton!"

Longarm wrote in his notebook as he asked if Eddy might by any chance be a Cornish name.

The foreman said, "I believe it is. But watch yourself around old Lyn Eddy, for by a name of any color he's a nasty one, look you!"

Chapter 15

California Gulch, southeast of Leadville, had been where the first color had been struck thereabouts. Placer gold mixed with heavy black sand reducing to forty or more ounces of silver a ton. But first find meant first mined and most of the California Gulch claims were bottomed out with weeds and lodgepole pine seedlings reclaiming tailing piles and the dooryards of rotting cabins.

Here and there eternal optimists or damned fools reworked abandoned claims. Recovery methods improved every season and running tailings that had worked in more haste in past summers could sometimes earn a man a living if he wasn't afraid of hard work.

High- or low-grade, crushed rock was heavy when wet, dusty and almost as heavy when dry. Nobody knew why some men dug clams for a living, or tried to breed earthworms for fun and profit either.

The Truro Mine had been the Luck of the Irish after it had been the Dream Girl after it had been Maggy's Mine after it had been a try hole sunk by the United States Geological Survey and written off by the government geologists as barren bedrock all the way to China.

So the antiquated Spanish arrastra dug in and lined with

stone to crush ore was a recent improvement, Longarm knew, as he dismounted out of rifle range of the skinny old man in a straw hat and bib overalls supervising the mule he had going around and around, hitched to a pivoting crossbar as it hauled a road builder's paving roller in an endless circle.

As Longarm watched the old man reached in the wheelbarrow he stood by to pick out and toss a lump of rock on the circular trench amid the smaller stones and grit the roller had already produced. Longarm tethered his livery mount to the sign reading, TRURO MINING COMPANY, PRIVATE PROPERTY! KEEP OUT! SURVIVORS WILL BE PROSECUTED!

As he walked down the gentle slope from the trace the old man turned with the Dance Dragoon he'd been holding down his far side to train it on Longarm, snarling, "Are you blind, illiterate, or just suicidal, you son of a bitch?"

Cornish folk had lost their old-time Celtic lingo earlier than the Welsh and Scots-Irish so they sounded about the same as other Lime Juicers. More like New Englanders than folk from the north of England, as the murderous Ben Thompson talked. Longarm had read how folk from the south of England had settled the northern states whilst folk from the north of England had settled the American South. He had no doubt the older man understood every word when he called back, "Cut the bullshit and listen tight. I am Deputy U.S. Marshal Custis Long of the Denver District Court but what you may or may not be doing here is betwixt you and the U.S. Geological Survey. I ain't paid to enforce no mining claims. Are you with me so far?"

Lyn Eddy said, "You got no right to come on my claim without a search warrant!"

Longarm said, "You ain't with me so far. We both know there's nothing to be searched for down that coyote

124

hole. I've come to offer you a deal. I can't make you agree to it. I can only make you wish to Christ your *had*."

Eddy lowered his dragoon back down to his side and decided. "We'd better talk about it in the shade. Grab a seat over on the porch and I'll be with you directly."

Longarm ambled over to the one-room cabin near the official adit to Eddy's hole in the ground and lit a cheroot before he sat in a barrel near a hopefully empty dynamite box.

The crusty receiver of stolen goods unhitched the mule to lead it out of the gritty stone-lined arrastra to rest its hooves on softer bare ground with a nose bag filled with water before he joined Longarm on his porch, grudgingly observing, "You're the one they call Longarm, ain't you? They tell me you're firm but fair. So what have you got to sell me?"

Longarm said, "I'd best start by putting my cards on the table, face up. If you don't like 'em you can shove 'em up your ass on your way to jail."

Eddy snorted. "I said I was listening. Could you spare one of those smokes?"

Longarm said, "Not yet. I follow the customs of Mister Lo, the poor Indian, when it comes to smoking with new faces. So shut your face and listen to my story. I was sent up here to Lake County on a federal case, which you ain't, even though I could likely prove you just took a whole wheelbarrow of high-grade out of that cobwebby coyote hole if I had me the *time*. So it's in the best interest of you and your fellow petty thieves to see me off soon as possible with my bigger case cracked."

Eddy bitched, "Watch who you're calling small time, pilgrim, the crushed ore in yonder arrastra figures to yield more silver than you make in a year! But keep talking."

Longarm did, bringing the old crook up to date on the confused case so far, stressing the matter of the shoot-out in the Taj Mahal, if you wanted to call it that, betwixt an

125

unprofessional lawman and a known enemy of an undetermined number of Cousin Jacks.

Eddy snorted. "A lot you know about high-grading. I have your word, as a man, we're having an unwitnessed conversation I'll never be asked to sign?"

Longarm said, "Learn me about high-grading."

So Eddy did. He admitted buying ore he asked no questions about once he'd tested it inside with his blow pipe. Different elements gave off different colors with a hot white flame played over them at a sharp angle. Once he accumulated about a wheelbarrowful from all over as the hard-won product of his Truro Mining Company, never having claimed he'd drilled, blasted, and mucked shit, he reduced it to that odd but high-grade of crushed ore until he had a couple of tons to dray on up to the smelter where, what do you know, it yielded better than anything Hod Tabor had ever produced from his famous Matchless Mine, the stuck-up son of a bitch.

As to Wig Gruber, another son of a bitch, being assassinated by the orders of business associates Eddy did not feel free to name, he could safely say that if nobody *missed* the son of a bitch, some of them had lost money on the deal.

When Longarm found that hard to follow, the bigger crook the smaller crooks carried their high-grade to explained, "There's no way to gather enough high-grade to matter at a well-guarded claim. That's why they hire tough sons of bitches to guard them. So tell me something if you know so much, Longarm: How would you go about picking fist-to-coconut-sized lumps from an ore pram and holding them up to the light to study, with a hairpin known to have killed high-graders in the past watching you?"

Longarm said, "You couldn't, if he was really watching you."

Eddy said, "There you go. Gruber was on the take. The

weak link in the chain them cheap Dutch fairies wrapped about their Warmerbroder was expecting any man, even a fellow Dutchman with a rep, to content himself with the five-hundred dollars a month they were paying him. All them rich sons of bitches feel that way about working stiffs who don't have money to throw at the birds whilst they put on a clean shirt every day. Every damned one of the mines in this district is sternly guarded by hard cases who beat the shit out of what you call petty thieves because the mine owners like to brag about their tight security. It just ain't worth the risk of an easy job to risk it for less than a quarter ton or so of purloined pebbles, if you follow my drift."

Longarm did. He marveled, "What you suggest is raw as hell, but so is raw ore, untraceable to a particular hole in the ground once you *cart* it away with the blessings of the security crew!"

Eddy said, "Ain't suggesting. Telling it like it is. Only two breeds of high-graders in any mining district. Bums who risk a beating for a little drinking money, and professionals who know how it's done. Gruber was a mean motherfucker willing to settle for a third of the weekly take. His replacement, another motherfucking Dutchman named Steiner, has been demanding a thicker slice. But it evens out because he ain't as experienced as Gruber was and it's easier to cheat him."

He smiled off in the distance and added, "Gruber wasn't getting as much as he thought, either. The smelter man he was paying to tally the final yield was a friend of mine, even if he was a dumb Taffy."

Longarm frowned thoughtfully and asked, "Are we talking about any Welshman on his day shift?"

Eddy said, "Graveyard shift. They run the smelters round the clock and . . . damn you're good! How did you guess that?"

Longarm said, "Fucked a Gypsy one night in the light

127

of the moon. So you're saying nobody you deal with would have had any call to pay a whole lot of money to have Wig Gruber killed?"

Eddy repeated his sensible observation about the crooked element among the local Cousin Jacks having had every reason to encourage the protracted existence of a fellow crook. So Longarm handed him a smoke and lit it for him before he rose with a thoughtful glance at the late afternoon sun and allowed he had to get it on down the road.

He returned the bronc to its livery after dropping by the Western Union to send a wire confessing he had no idea what he was doing up in Leadville. Then he ambled over to the card house annex of the Taj Mahal to scout up the notorious Johnny Dart. For if the high-graders hadn't paid Grant Webber handsomely for gunning Wig Gruber he'd either won the price of that pig farm in that now-legendary card game or he'd come by sudden prosperity some other way.

He bellied up to the bar in the card house and ordered something cool to relax the barkeep some before he pestered him. After idly chatting, Longarm allowed he'd missed their famous draw poker showdown betwixt the famous Johnny Dart and that wanted murderer, Grant Webber.

The barkeep looked uncomfortable, said he'd been off that night, and polished his way out of earshot along the bar.

He left half of his beer behind, and strode back out in the late afternoon sunlight. The wine theater next door wasn't open yet. The banks and other public offices were closed for the day. He strolled back to his hotel for an early supper and to see if there were any messages for him.

There was one. The Powerful Patricia's perfumed note

128

suggested he drop by the Carbonate Spa later that evening because she had something to show him.

He had something to show her, too, after recovering from the effects of crib seventeen in a rival establishment. But she'd said to drop by later in the evening and all that riding in the thin mountain air had sharpened his appetite. So, heeding the advice young Queen Victoria had been given by the Archbishop on her way to be crowned, Longarm ambled in to the hotel restaurant again.

The fatherly Archbishop had warned her young majesty not ever to miss a chance to get off her feet, grab a meal, or take a piss. It was not too clear how the details of this conversation had gotten around, but it was still good advice.

The pleasantly plump, redheaded Lilo was still on duty and beginning to look as if she could have used the same advice. Longarm didn't know her well enough to tell her to go take a piss, but once he'd ordered the same blue plate with a side order of *huevos ranchero* for variety he suggested, "You got no more than half an hour before the evening rush begins, Miss Lilo. I know the feeling and it might help if you found some place in the back to lay down and put your legs up."

She wearily asked, "With whom do you suggest?"

Longarm smiled up sheepishly and said, "I was only trying to help, Miss Lilo. I wasn't flirting with you."

She sighed, "I know," and softly murmured, "Damn it!" as she turned away sharply. He figured they were at the stage of the game where she was starting to wonder why he wasn't more forward, or if he was even interested in her.

He was, but he wasn't. The Powerful Patricia was a bird in the hand and she'd said she had something to show him, but it sure beat all how women along about sundown commenced to remind a man of ducks.

A man could sit all afternoon in a duck blind with his shotgun up and never see duck one. Then, just as you'd get one to aim at, a whole flock would flutter into range and *then* what was a man supposed to do?

Chapter 16

Longarm tried for Johnny Dart with no luck at the Taj Mahal another time and mosied on up to the Carbonate Spa as State Street was getting its stride after sundown. He found an empty table near the back and took a seat. The shapely brunette waitress heading his way to take his order wasn't the Powerful Patricia. Longarm was good at faces but it took him a moment to recognize her in that getup.

He said, "Evening, Miss Cherry. I like what you've done to your hair. It used to be blond, right?"

Cherry Poppins smiled down at him to reply, "It was Miss Patricia's notion when I asked her if I could work for her instead of Madame Three Tits. She said I'd likely make less a night, working harder, and when I still said I wanted to be a fucking lady she said we'd better make it tougher for my old admirerers to recognize me. That's what Miss Patricia calls gents who've fucked me. 'Admirerers.' I ain't supposed to serve nobody sitting alone at one of these tables, Custis. But seeing you've been fucking one of the owners I reckon it will be all right. What can I fetch you?"

He said she'd best bring him a carafe of Chablis, seeing

131

the house stood to make as much that way than if a couple ordered Dago Red. She said she'd see they poured it from a jug of the real Chablis and left to fetch it.

Longarm leaned back to light a smoke. The place was still half empty, as was the orchestra pit with the stage lights dark as that asbestos curtain promised in writing to cure what ailed you. He'd just gotten his cheroot going when a cadaverous individual who looked as if he'd put on his own undertaker's rusty black suit and shoestring tie loomed over him to say, "Take it over to the bar, Uncle Sam. Just because you pack a badge gives you no right to hog a whole table with one lonesome ass!"

Longarm took a thoughtful drag, blew smoke at the older and skinnier cuss, and soberly replied, "If you know who I am you know who you're fucking with. But you have the advantage on me. Who the fuck are you?"

The rusty black suit replied, "Hawkins, R. R. Hawkins, and that's my table you're tying up with the curtain fixing to go up. I own a one-third interest in this place and you don't scare me with your *guns* and glowers because I am within my rights and you'd best just move that ass like I told you!"

Longarm said, "Aw, shit, don't get your bowels in an uproar, third pard, I ordered Chablis with the upkeep of this joint in mind."

Hawkins said, "I don't care if you ordered champagne over out-of-season strawberries! You ain't sitting alone at that table!"

Then Cherry Poppins was back with his order and, better yet, the Powerful Patricia, who subtly but firmly told Hawkins, "Deputy Long is an invited guest, Roy. I asked him to join me here this evening."

Hawkins sneered. "In that case why don't you take him upstairs and fuck him?"

Before she could answer Longarm was up from his seat at the table and Roy Hawkins was on his way down. Men

132

usually went down when a man Longarm's size cold-cocked them with a hard left. As Hawkins landed in the sawdust on his rusty black bottom the Powerful Patricia was between them with both hands against Longarm's tweed vest, urgently pleading, "Let it go, Custis! He's the asshole I told you about the other night! He means no harm. He's simply stupid!"

"He has a big mouth, too," Longarm quietly observed as Cherry Poppins asked where they wanted her to put that carafe of Chablis.

As the Powerful Patricia took it from her and advised her to skoot, Roy Hawkins rose on one knee, holding one hand to his face as he told the sawdust he was staring down at, "I'm going to sue the government if this bone is really broken."

The Powerful Patricia said, "Roy, go away, or I'll turn this guy loose on you. You've said enough already, you poor simp!"

Cherry Poppins helped the part owner up to his feet. He shrugged her off and stormed out of sight as more than one of the regulars stared after him with bemused smiles.

The Powerful Patricia set the carafe on the table and took a seat. Longarm sat down in the chair he'd popped up from. He told her he was sorry for acting without thinking. She said, "I heard what he said. He had it coming and I'm glad you popped him. I just didn't want you putting him in the hospital. My other partner, the sane one I mentioned the other night, has threatened to pick up his marbles and go home, or, worse yet, sell his shares to August Rische if Roy gets into anymore scrapes with his big mouth and ever-erect libido."

Longarm said, "I was wondering what was eating old Roy. I didn't, ah, come between the two of you the other night, I hope?"

The Powerful Patricia sniffed. "God will get you for

133

that! The poor simp's been trying to get up my skirts since first we met. But as I told him long before I ever laid eyes on you, I'd sleep with the fat but rich Prince of Wales, first, if I was in the habit of sleeping with married men, rich or poor. You may find this hard to buy, considering some of the things I've said to you in the past, dog style, but I do have *some* moral standards, Custis."

He poured white wine for both of them as he soberly agreed. "Most of us do and if I ever sleep with a married woman she won't be married up with my business partner. You say your *third* partner seems to be on to old Roy?"

She nodded and said, "As I told you, Will Travis keeps his thoughts and his private life to himself. He seldom comes around, being largely interested in the books he keeps on this and other holdings here in Leadville. When he heard about Roy getting into it with a customer over the customer's own lady friend, he warned Roy he didn't mean to warn him again. So we're not going to bother Will about what just happened, are we?"

Longarm said, "My lips are sealed, as long as Roy keeps his mouth shut around this child. Will Travis selling out to the biggest Dutchman in Leadville would be, what, malice aforethought?"

She sighed and said, "You know it. August Rische would love to be one up on his own old partner, Hod Tabor, in this part of town. Sometimes I fear the two factions have lost sight of the profit motive and just like to stick pins in one another!"

She took but a sip of her Chablis, rose, and leaned over to give him a peck on the cheek, saying, "Stick around," before she left him there, to vanish into the smokey gloom of the cavernous wine theater.

Longarm muttered, "So what was it she wanted to show me, then?"

His cheroot had gone out. He relit it to make his wine last, not so much to save money as to stay sober with the night so young and the jealous Roy Hawkins prowling round out there in all that cigar smoke.

A young kid in overalls was crawling across the stage, lighting the footlights, as the musicians filed into the orchestra pit, looking as if they were already exhausted. But once they'd tuned up, one of them laughing like a jackass about something, they struck up that tune about the Bowery in New York City and the curtain rose to reveal a pathetic little flower girl, of no more than forty, who wailed, as the musicians backed off,

> "Who will buy me fresh blooming lavender?
> Sixteen branches for a penny?
> You buy 'em once you'll buy 'em twice!
> They make your clothes smell bloody nice!"

Her accent, as well as her English music hall song, was pure John Bull, in spite of where she was that evening. It was safe to say a heap of the customers at the other tables were, too. Cousin Jack was the star of hard-rock mining, once you got down below the loose ore and had to drill where a slip of your star-bit could scald you like a lobster in boiling water or bring the mountain down on your head.

Unless you were a Dutchman, working another slower but safer ancient mining tradition. But you expected to find Leadville's digging Dutchmen in places like the Lorelei, not places like this one or the Taj Mahal.

So what business had the late Wig Gruber being in the Taj Mahal barroom when Grant Webber shot him, fair and square or down and dirty? Wig Gruber had known he was unpopular with the boys from Britain. He should have felt as awkward there as a Protestant at a Polish wedding.

"Payoff," Longarm decided. Old Lyn Eddy had said Gruber had been paid to look the other way as his absentee owners played slap and tickle. So Grant Webber, being

135

a local lawman, had heard the same gossip and simply had to lay in wait where a corrupt security man was in the habit of . . .

"Why, sure!" Longarm told his wine glass as he raised it to his lips, "The last place a crooked Dutchman would have secret meetings with high-graders would be some place *Dutch* mining men hung out! Wig Gruber could have danced on the bar in the Taj Mahal without his fellow Dutchmen ever noticing. But Grant Webber was paid to prowl *all* the joints along State Street—Anglo, Dutch, or in between!"

He sipped some Chablis, which tasted sort of like calmed-down champagne, and muttered, "That ain't all that much of an elimination. We're still stuck with the big question: Who paid Grant Webber if it wasn't the Cousin Jacks Wig Gruber was working with on the sly?"

Longarm tensed inside his own skin as he became aware of another figure looming over him in the smoky gloom, with all the serious lamp light on that little flower girl of forty.

Then he saw it was Mart Duggan in the flashy flesh and said, "Take a load off your feet and have some of this expensive watered wine. I take it you've something to say, Mart?"

The town marshal sat down where the Powerful Patricia's far more desirable rump had reposed, to say, "I don't drink that French piss. First off, the coroner's jury and county prosecuter agree Grant Webber beat his common-law wife to death and they'd sworn out a bill of indictment on the miserable son of a bitch. After that he was spotted boarding the narrow gauge for Denver the next day, long before you reported the murder to Lake County and all."

"Want me to wire Denver P.D. for you?" Longarm asked.

Duggan snorted, "Don't teach your granny to suck

eggs. Lake County put out an all points already. How did you think *Leadville* P.D. knows so much? By the time you found those kids alone out there with a mother rotting under a haystack the cocksucker who killed her would have had time to get laid at Ruth Jacob's joint in Denver and still hop a train on out to anywhere!"

Longarm grimaced and decided, "It happens that way, sometimes. We can't win 'em all. If he got away clean with what's left of that payroll money I told you about, I'm just up your way for the thin dry air mixed with smelter fumes. Doc Holiday allowed it was good for his own lungs when he was terrorizing your town."

Duggan said, "I'll thank you to note Doc Holiday and Soapy Smith left Leadville when I took over as town marshal!"

Longarm shrugged and said, "Whatever. I ain't packing federal warrants on them, either. The present whereabouts of Grant Webber ain't none of my beeswax if all he did was assassinate Wig Gruber for profit and kill his woman for fun. It *is* my beeswax if he just shot a wanted man for a modest reward and recovered that fifty grand of Uncle Sam's without a word about it to Uncle Sam. I sure would like to talk to the son of a bitch. Because it works out as well either way!"

Duggan warned, "If you ever do meet up with Grant Webber, make sure you throw down on him before you ask him any questions. He's one mean son of a bitch and it's established he was fast enough to take Web Gruber, face-to-face."

Longarm pointed out, "Gruber wasn't expecting a man he knew as one of your lawmen to draw on him."

Duggan said, "Just the same, it took more guts, and more speed, than your average son of a bitch would have. Wig Gruber had a rep, the same as you. So we ain't talking about a wild kid here. Webber is the real deal. So take my advice if you do run into Grant Webber as you drift through life. Shoot the son of a bitch. Serious. Before you try to question him."

The town tamer smiled as if in fond memory as he added, "They talk more freely when they're dying, anyhow."

Longarm said, "You're all heart. You said that was the *first* thing we had to talk about, Mart?"

Duggan said, "They say Johnny Dart has put out the word he's ready when you are. Somebody told him you'd been asking about him, speaking of hot-tempered pains in the ass. He packs a double action Starr thirty-eight in a shoulder holster. You can see a front strap across his brocaded vest. I have already put out word of my own that if he's dumb enough to draw on a federal lawman, premeditated, I'll kill him if you fail to. I won't put up with that sort of shit in *my* town!"

Longarm thanked his fellow lawman for the tip but added, "Things may not be that serious. I've only told others who know him I wanted a word with him. Some troublemaker may be putting words in both our faces in the hope of seeing some fireworks. I wish they wouldn't do that. But it goes with our job."

Duggan rose to go on about his own business. Longarm finished what was left in his glass and rose to his feet with his cheroot gripped in his teeth, leaving the rest of his wine to whomever wanted it. On his way out he met up with Cherry Poppins near the front. He asked her to tell the Powerful Patricia he might or might not be coming back sort of late.

The recently reformed harlot asked if he was meeting up with some other woman on the side. She hadn't been reformed that long. He told her, "I've been invited to a friendly conversation or a showdown with another man. Like the old church song says, 'Farther along we'll know all about it.' "

" 'Farther along we'll understand why'!" the new brunette trilled up at him, adding, "I used to go to church when I was little and still thought there was somebody in charge of all this shit."

Longarm laughed and went on out to State Street, crowding up now, as Leadville's nightlife put away enough joy juice to start feeling frisky.

When he got to the Taj Mahal card house he took a deep breath and stepped inside with his pocket derringer palmed in one fist. But when he moved over to the bar along one wall to ask the barkeep where Johnny Dart might be, the worried-looking employee said, "He's been in and out all evening, getting drunker as he prowls State Street for somebody he seems to be mad as hell at."

He added, in a desperately polite tone, "I sure hope you ain't him, Mister."

Chapter 17

Longarm would have stood pat in Johnny Dart's place of business if a waitress from the wine theater next door hadn't come in to tell him her boss wanted a word with him.

Longarm told the barkeep to tell Johnny Dart he'd be back. Then he followed the shapely young thing through a side door into the gloom beyond, where another veteran of the English music halls was inviting one and all to come up in her balloon.

The waitress led Longarm up the stairs he'd mounted earlier with Freedom Ford. They traversed the same tiled corridor past that storeroom full of fermenting ginger beer to what looked to be just a door until you stepped inside to find yourself in some degenerate Turk's notion of his seventh heaven.

His guide in harem costume shut the door after her as she left him in the presence of a Hindu maharani posed like that caterpillar on a mushroom in *Alice in Wonderland*. However, in this case the mushroom was a mighty pile of velvet pillows and the lady lounging atop of it as she smoked a bubble pipe was shaped a lot more interesting than any caterpillar Longarm had ever seen.

Swathed in scarlet silk sari cloth, she had snow-white hair but one of those ageless faces a capricious fate bestows on some women whether they deserve it or not. As she blew a cloud of hashish smoke his way Longarm somehow doubted she worried all that much about staying in shape. She likely got other exercise.

Her voice, when she spoke, was a pleasant contralto with foundations of Cornish granite under the brick-college accent of the British East India Company's management staff. She said, "Allow me to introduce myself, Deputy Long. I am Binnie Bodmin, the owner of all you survey on this block. You may call me Binnie because I do so hope we shall be friends."

Longarm doffed his hat to her and replied, "In that case you can call me Custis, because all my friends do, Miss Binnie."

She patted the pile she lounged on and invited him to climb aboard as she said, "I can't afford another shooting on my premises down below, Custis. I have my own ways of dealing with Johnny Dart. Their names are Phyllis and Fran. They'll get word to us when it's safe for you to show your face outside again."

Longarm said, "That's mighty big of you, Miss Binnie. But I *want* to meet up with this Johnny Dart. I have questions to ask him about that other shooting downstairs."

She took a drag on her bubble pipe, lay back to spout smoke up at her ceiling of carved and gilded cheeseboard, and insisted, "You don't understand. Nobody talks to Johnny Dart when he's drunk and defending his honor. He doesn't want to talk to you about that legendary game of draw poker with Grant Webber. Johnny prides himself on never lying, so he'd as soon kill you as admit the truth."

"Might anybody else around here know the truth?" asked Longarm.

The sultry white-haired belle of India rolled up on one

elbow. Her shoulder and half a tit on that side were suddenly exposed to the moody light of her seventh heaven when loose red silk repositioned itself, as it was no doubt meant to. She said, "It never happened. Trust me. I *own* the card house the legendary game is said to have taken place in."

Longarm braced himself on one arm, his palm planted on a pillow that felt just like a big tit, to ask, "You mean Grant Webber didn't win as much as he let on, playing cards with the famous Johnny Dart?"

She sniffed and said, "I mean they never played cards at all. Grant Webber was a lawman and perhaps a paid assassin. He was never known as a sporting man. He never won a dime off Johnny Dart or anyone else in my card house. I asked. My help knows better than to fib to me."

Longarm frowned down on her, since she was on her back blowing smoke at the ceiling again, and said, "I'm missing something here. If Grant Webber got all that money somewheres else, and told a big fib about winning it off the famous Johnny Dart, how come Johnny Dart never called him on it?"

Binnie Bodmin calmly asked, "Would you play cards with a famous gambler who never lost? As Grant Webber knew, his spreading word that Johnny Dart could be beaten, big time, was good for Johnny's business! He's been making money hand over fist, playing high rollers out to top the big win of Grant Webber!"

Longarm thought, smiled thinly, and said, "Nobody likes to buck a tiger that can't be tamed. Lots of professionals face that problem. Why do they call him Johnny Dart? Is he supposed to be sharp, or what?"

She said, "Dart is his last name. He's a Cousin Jack, you see, or he was until he found he had a natural talent at the card table and gave up *drilling* for silver. Dart is a common Cornish surname. Why don't you take off your hat and coat, and *must* you wear a gun to bed with a lady?"

He tossed his pancaked Stetson aside, but let it go at that as he told her he hadn't been aware they were supposed to be in bed together.

She smiled up at him, blew a hashish smoke ring at him, and confided, "I'd heard about you and us girls before I listened outside crib seventeen as you were trying to split that sweet young thing like firewood, to hear her moaning and groaning. But you don't have to make love to me if you find me too . . . mature for you. Just stay here where you'll be safe 'til my other sweet young things have Johnny Dart calmed down."

Longarm shook his head and said, "Whether or not he lost all that money to Grant Webber is only one of the things I want to ask him. I ain't out to expose any professional secrets on him. He can have it known he can be taken, if that's his pleasure. But if Grant Webber never won all that money downstairs he was either *paid* all that money by somebody else or he *stole* all that money somewhere else, and . . . I may as well level with you, Miss Binnie. He may have stolen it *upstairs* in one of your cribs or that storeroom with a wooden floor."

She chuckled and trilled, "So Joy was right. That *was* you striking matches in there the other night. What am I supposed to be hiding from you under those floorboards, or anywhere else?"

He said, "I ain't accusing you of hiding nothing, Miss Binnie. You must have heard how they arrested the late Abner Prentiss, the bank robber, just up the way?"

She covered a yawn with the back of her manicured hand and replied, "Oh, him? He only stayed with us one night, in crib fourteen as a matter of fact. I didn't know he was a bank robber when I asked him to take his custom up the street. I only thought he was loony, asking one of my girls to be the girl he left behind, even though she'd never seen him before."

Longarm said, "He found the gal of his dreams at another establishment up the street. Crib fourteen, you say he stayed in, Miss Binnie?"

She said, "Yes. The money's not there. In India we used to pour water on the dirt floors Thugi bandits might have stayed in. As the dirt began to dry you could see were it had been dug up in the past. As soon as I heard we'd had a famous bank robber with us overnight I had my help completely refinish crib fourteen. He didn't pussyfoot along the corridor to hide it among my ginger beer, either. I had *those* floorboards pried up the morning after you aroused my suspicious nature with your pungent Mexican matches."

He smiled sheepishly and said, "At least they're waterproof. It ain't as if I'm a trusting moon calf, Miss Binnie. But even if you recovered the loot it wouldn't be there now. So I reckon I have to take your word it ain't."

She demurely asked, "Would you care to search *me*, then?" and before he could say that hardly seemed sensible she'd flung a whole lot of red scarlet silk aside and the notion of at least looking her over made a whole lot of sense. For despite her hair being white all over, she was built like that marble statue of Venus, except she was holding two shapely arms out to him as she said huskily, "I haven't a thing I don't want you . . . investigating."

So, being a natural man and not wanting to make a mortal enemy of a likely dangerous woman, he thought it best not to get her all riled up and feeling scorned when all you had to do to calm things down only required a man to do those things that came natural.

As they kissed whilst all four of their hands proceeded to undress him, Longarm felt a light buzz from her hashish-scented breath and hoped she wasn't going to accuse him, later, of taking advantage of her bubble pipe.

Then she'd taken the matter in hand to work it harder and steer him betwixt her welcoming thighs. As he parted her prematurely white pubic hair with his old organ grinder he decided she was one hell of an actress or really didn't put out to just anybody, as she said, as they got going serious. If she was conning him, that was fair, for he was conning her and it sure felt swell, even as he idly wondered how he figured to save some for later with the Powerful Patricia. He knew the big athletic brunette was awaiting this same pleasure as he was pleasuring this shorter, softer, older gal. Knowing he was being sort of a rotter to the both of them filled him and his old organ grinder with mixed emotions. You could see how some gents enjoyed a roll in the alley with some unwashed slut whilst their loving wives kept supper in the oven for them. He could tell Binnie Bodmin was enjoying herself a heap as her wet innards pulsated around his questing manhood. He wondered why she was conning him. He knew he was only . . . aw, shit, doing what any other man would have done when a good-looking woman wasn't actually fending him off. So maybe she was telling the truth and simply liked to get laid.

It could happen.

The trouble after that was Grant Webber's story, and he wasn't in Leadville any more. Whether he'd been paid a fortune to kill that Dutchman, or found the damned money where Abner Prentiss had hidden it was tumbleweeding its way to a moot question. You couldn't ask a man who wasn't within miles, or recently hanged. Longarm couldn't think of anybody else who'd know.

Binnie wanted to show him some secrets of the *Kama Sutra*, the Hindu love manual most everyone who'd ever been in a dirty book store had already looked at. But he was a good sport and acted surprised when she coyly got on top with her legs in what she described as a lotus position. It looked wilder than it felt. That was the trouble

145

with suggestions in the *Kama Sutra*. They'd been made up by a Hindu with a pencil in one hand and his own fool pecker in the other. Real naked bodies didn't work that way.

She agreed it might feel better if she let him back on top. But as they settled in for more that way, the stuff she'd been smoking caught up with her and Longarm found himself fornicating with Sleeping Beauty. He'd have finished in her anyway, being human, if he hadn't had a live one waiting up State Street for it. He hauled it out hard, wiped it dry on scarlet silk, and got dressed again to keep his midnight tryst with the Powerful Patricia.

It was going on 10:30 as he mosied up State Street. So he was fairly sure he'd be able to rise to the occasion by midnight as long as he laid off the sauce.

Little Cherry Poppins had been watching for him near the entrance of the Carbonate Spa. As he strolled in she grabbed him by a sleeve to haul him off to one side, saying, "I've been so worried about you! A mean-looking cuss is in the bar, talking ugly about you and poor Miss Patricia with Roy Hawkins. It ain't true that the two of you think you're so much better than the rest of us. You and Miss Patricia have treated me like a fucking lady!"

He chuckled. "Well, ain't you a fucking lady, Miss Cherry? I know what's eating Hawkins. Might this other galoot be wearing a brocaded vest and answering to the name of Johnny?"

She said, "That's what Roy Hawkins called him! He came in drunk and Roy's been treating him to free drinks at the bar. What's it about, Custis? Why is the one called Johnny sore at you?"

Longarm said, "I'll ask him. I hope it's just one of those mixups you get when gents who crave excitement get to egging on a mean drunk. I want you to stay here, Miss

146

Cherry. It's distracting to worry about others in the line of fire."

He moved on into the smoke-filled darkness along the wall of the wine theater as up on the stage the footlights illuminated a not-bad-looking gal dressed like Calamity Jane or Poker Alice as she spun a trick rope pretty good. Mining men were more impressed than the gents in a cow town might have been.

Longarm spotted the familiar rusty black figure of Roy Hawkins at the bar with another gent in a white planter's hat and light-gray frock coat. Hawkins spotted Longarm at the same time and said something. Johnny Dart swung away from the bar and spun on one heel to face him as Longarm called out, "Simmer down and listen up, old son! We ain't at feud. I ain't fixing to give away any trade secrets. I know you don't know anything I need to know and—"

And then Johnny Dart was going for his double action and, as everybody knows, there is just no way a man packing cross-draw on his hip is about to beat a man on the prod with his hand already streaking for his shoulder holster.

Not unless the intended victim has been forewarned, least ways.

Johnny Dart, in spite of being drunk as hell, was still faster than your average gun-slick. So it must have surprised the shit out him in the time he had left to take one round just over the heart, and a second smack dab, as Longarm fired the double derringer he'd been palming since Cherry Poppins had *told* him there was an asshole in the bar making war talk.

As the gunsmoke cleared to reveal Johnny Dart's form at the feet of Roy Hawkins, the rat-faced troublemaker spread his hands wide when he bleated, "I'm not carrying! It was his idea, not mine, on my mother's honor!"

By then Longarm had his more serious .44–40 out to

147

cover everybody as he sneered, "You never had no mother. A coyote pissed on a pile of shit and the sun hatched you out. I'm holding you as a material witness and you can explain what a good boy you are to the coroner's jury if you live that long. Say one more word before I cool down some and I doubt like hell you *will*, you two-faced yellow dog!"

Chapter 18

In no time at all the Carbonate Spa was as warm with other lawmen, Leadville and Lake County, and to his dubious credit, there being at least two dozen other witnesses, part owner Roy Hawkins agreed the dead drunk spread face up on the sawdust like an inverted bear rug had announced his intention to kill Longarm on sight and gone for his own gun first.

Cherry Poppins confirmed she'd heard Johnny Dart pissing and moaning that Longarm was after him. Longarm could only say he hadn't been and still had no idea what had gotten into the poor dead simp.

During a lull in the conversation the Powerful Patricia took Longarm to one side to introduce him to her other partner, the portly and balding Will Travis, and without ever saying so, let Longarm know she didn't have anything to show him upstairs after all, that evening. He assured her he understood. She suddenly looked as if butter wouldn't melt in her mouth. Longarm idly wondered how much the poker-faced Will Travis knew. A poker-faced cuss with partners like he had likely wished they'd both grow up a piece.

By midnight they'd taken the body away and the confusion seemed to be breaking up. One of the deputy coroners told Longarm not to leave town before the hearing. An assistant district attorney had him sign a shorthand deposition. Nobody seemed to think he was in trouble. But he knew Billy Vail was going to be mighty pissed.

He walked over to the all-night Western Union to send out a night letter spelling the unusual turn of events before he went back to his hotel to find the restaurant closed. So he went upstairs hungry and as he undressed and treated himself to a whore bath at the corner stand he swore at his fool pecker and said, "Don't blame *me* for what just happened! I thought we were acting smart when we quit whilst we were ahead at the Taj Mahal!"

The redheaded Lilo didn't come on until noon. So he ordered ham and eggs with a side order of chili off a plainer waitress. He was working on it when the distinguished lady journalist, Freedom Ford, joined him with her notebook and a sheepish smile. She said she'd been awfully busy since her byline had appeared all over the West and a couple of places back East, but intimated she'd been sort of missing him over to her places and allowed she might be receiving that evening if he cared to sup with her.

He honestly replied, "I ain't certain I'll be in town. The county wants me to stick around for their protracted paperwork, I ride for the federal government, and my boss drinks with Governor Pitkin. So I figure on coming back for the coroner's inquest once they set a date for the same."

She said, "But Custis, you have yet to solve the mystery of that missing money! Surely you have to stay until you do, right?"

He replied, "Wrong. We only have so many man hours to work any case and this one's cooled off to what we call an open case. We'll keep the missing money in mind. But we can't spend pounds to recover pence and there ain't nobody left to question up here in Lake County with Grant Webber Lord knows where and both Abner Prentiss and Johnny Dart dead."

She said she didn't see how the late Johnny Dart fit anywhere in the puzzle.

Longarm said, "Welcome to the club. I've been trying to make sense of what happened ever since it happened. I never thought Johnny Dart had the money. I only wanted him to confirm or deny Webber's claim he'd won that money in a card game instead of finding it under floorboards in . . . never mind. Some details are best played close to the vest, even when you ain't sure what you're playing with whom."

She scampered off to file her "interview." Longarm suspected that, like other reporters he'd been willing to have a cup of coffee with, she was fixing to build his simple self-defense against a mean drunk into a legend to rival the *Iliad*.

On his way back to the Western Union Longarm met up with Marshal Mart Duggan, who said, "I heard. You done good. Johnny Dart's real name was Edwin Drake and he was wanted in Nevada for a similar lapse of judgment, in which case he *beat* his man to the draw. We just got that in answer to the all-points we sent out last night. We ain't slow up here in Leadville, Denver boy!"

Longarm whistled softly and said, "Thus a guilty conscience doth make assholes of us all. When he heard a lawman from out of town had been asking for him he put two and two together to come up with six."

Duggan said, "Sure looks that way. You figure he was in on the killing of Wig Gruber after all?"

Longarm said, "Not hardly. I got it from other sources Webber just made up that famous card game to account for sudden wealth. Old Johnny Dart, or Drake, just lucked out last night and Webber seems to be long gone. I'm on my way to the telegraph office in the hope my home office agrees I've chased my tail around your city long enough."

Duggan asked, "What about the coroner's inquest on Dart?"

Longarm said, "Only takes a few hours either way on the narrow gauge and my boss is a slave driver. If he can't wiggle me off the hook entire I can always come back when and if your county pencil pushers set some damned date."

They shook and parted friendly. Longarm found no messages waiting when he got to the Western Union. He had a drink across the way and tried again. Billy Vail had wired for him to pack it in for now and come on back to Denver.

So he returned to his hotel to pick up his light baggage and check out. Knowing the Denver-bound narrow gauge wouldn't be leaving until noon he took his time—all the while resisting the temptation to say improper good-byes to any of the ladies in town he knew, in the biblical sense—to board the rinky-dink little passenger coach and scout for a seat. He knew it served him right for not boarding earlier.

Then a familiar voice yoo-hooed him to an empty seat beside her and as he sat down he asked the pleasantly plump redhead from his hotel restaurant what she was doing aboard a Denver-bound train.

Lilo said, "Going to Denver, of course. I just quit at the hotel. I have a better job lined up in the big city. I start next Monday at a fancy Bavarian beer garden out along Colfax Avenue."

Longarm said, "I think I know the place. They unload a lot of beer and sausage, being out on that streetcar line in a Dutch neighborhood. Where were you fixing on staying when you first get in to Denver?"

When she said she wasn't certain, and meant to check in near the railroad depot, Longarm told her he could steer her better than that. So they talked about it a lot and

152

rubbed legs a mite and wound up sort of holding hands by the time they rolled into Denver later that afternoon. So it seemed only natural, once they had her settled in a clean hotel that wasn't going to cost her an arm and a leg, to sort of wind up testing the bedsprings.

They didn't squeak worth mention, she turned out to be redheaded all over, and, thanks to all the honest toil she'd been putting in, a lot more solid than one might think, looking at her with her clothes on. As they paused for a smoke whilst resting up from those first wild fumbles it takes a couple to make friends, it was just starting to get dark out. Lilo laughed and said she'd meant to hold out until after he treated her to a set-down supper where *she* got to order.

He allowed he'd somehow worked up an appetite and suggested that as the evening was still young they might as well get dressed and go have that set-down supper before he showed her some positions he'd seen in this Hindu love manual.

Lilo thought that was a grand notion and warned him once he put a little beer and sausage in her that there was just no telling what she'd want him putting in her next.

So they got up and got dressed and even though he offered to take her to Romano's or the exotic Golden Dragon, both closer, Lilo wanted to ride the infernal streetcar out to that Bavarian beer garden and look the place over as a customer before she started serving there.

It made sense. Once the horse-drawn streetcar had them up the sort-of-scary slope of Capitol Hill it didn't take long before Longarm spied the green copper spire of that Dutch Papist church and so they got off to follow the sound of an oompah-pah quartet up the block to the beer garden surrounded by a whitewashed trellis and decorated with paper lanterns that were just commencing to glow against the lavender sky of the gloaming.

They went on in. Longarm felt a tad left out as Lilo

153

spoke in Dutch to a younger gal in a Dutch peasant dress as she led them to their table. As they sat down Lilo allowed she was going to enjoy working there. The couples at the other tables were her kind of folk. Longarm had to be a good sport about it. He'd been the only Anglo at more than one fiesta, though he savvied more border Mex than Dutch.

After that it seemed easier to fit in as long as you kept your fool mouth shut. Most folk of northern European ancestry looked a lot the same. Those who looked peculiarly English, Irish, Dutch, or whatever probably hailed from inbred backwaters. As he gazed idly about Longarm noticed some few, blond squareheaded types who looked the way Dutch folk were supposed to. Here and there at the other tables you'd see that other extreme but just as Dutch-looking swarthy black-haired sort. A couple at a nearby table made him wonder where he'd seen them before. When he looked right at them the brown-haired, brown-eyed gal looked like dozens of Dutch gals he'd had pointed out to him in the past. Her escort looked as if he needed a shave and his black beetle brows met in the middle. But after that when he laughed at something the gal had said he didn't have any gold teeth.

Lilo ordered for them from a menu that could have been printed in Greek as far as Longarm could tell. She said they were fixing to dine on sour beef and potato dumplings if that was all right with him. He told her that sounded fine and asked if she knew what sort of name *Webber* might be.

She said, "Dutch, of course. It would be *Weaver* in English. Why do you ask?"

He said, "That bird across the way would answer the description of a man wanted by Lake County for murder, and by Uncle Sam for questioning, if only he were a tad older and had a gold tooth. I sure feel dumb. It just never occured to me that Webber might not be a regular American name. I've met more than one Webber and none of them struck me odd."

She said, "Thank you."

He said, "I don't mean *ugly* odd. I just meant Dutch. Grant Webber strangled a woman of Scots-Irish descent he gunned down another *Dutchman* named Gruber and like a fool I suspected Webber might be a regular English name."

Their order came. It was hearty fare that stuck to the ribs and he liked the beer they washed it down with, too. They had what surely could have passed for American apple pie with rat trap cheese for dessert and then he took her home to her hotel where a good time was had by all until he had to get on over to the federal building to report in the next morning.

When he told Billy Vail what he'd guessed about Grant Webber being a Dutchman, likely lying low amid his own kind in one of Denver's High or Low Dutch enclaves, Billy Vail said, "You'll never in this world do it alone. You don't talk Dutch and even if you did he'd likely make a break for it as soon as he heard strangers were asking about a beetle-browed regular with a gold tooth."

Longarm said, "Hold on, Webber ain't no regular. He's a new face in *Denver's* Dutch circles. Up until recent he was a regular in *Leadville*. So, what if Denver lawmen with familiar faces, speaking Dutch—?"

Billy Vail said, "Let's posse up and ride! I drink with Denver P.D. and they have more Dutchmen on the force than you can shake a stick at. You go on down the hall and report to Judge Dickerson for courtroom duty this morning. I want you where you can't get in trouble for the next few days."

Longarm frowned and demanded, "What are you talking about? Are you taking me off my own case?"

Vail nodded curtly and said, "Damned A, I am! Use your head, old son. You don't speak Dutch, and worse yet it was in the papers how you, the famous Longarm, discoved the body of Webber's murdered woman! If you so much as fart within a furlong of the bastard he's going to be long gone before the air clears."

Longarm didn't answer.

Vail said, "Don't pull a long face on me. You know I'm right."

To which Longarm could only reply, "That don't make it feel one lick better. What about that coroner's inquest up Lake County way?"

Vail said, "When the coroner calls it, you grab a train and get it on up yonder. Your shootout with Johnny Dart, alias Drake, has no bearing on the murder of Edith Webber, or for that matter the missing federal funds. If Webber lifted it we'll ask him where it is. If Webber ain't got it, it's gone. Can't spend more than Prentiss stole to recover what Prentiss stole. What are you waiting for, a kiss goodbye?"

Longarm cussed his way out to the hall and followed it on down to the shit chore Vail had saddled him with.

The hell of it was, he knew Billy Vail was right. There just came times a man had to admit he couldn't walk on water or pull rabbits out of his hat. But he thought it was really shitty of Billy Vail to forbid him to go anywhere near that beer garden Lilo was serving at, lonesome, for the moment.

But orders were orders. So he was having lo mein in the Golden Dragon with another gal entire when Deputy Bill Schneider shot Grant Webber in the *Frülingszeit* Saloon on Larimer Street. Deputy Schneider said he'd had to shoot the muley son of a bitch when he refused to come quietly.

Grant Webber had never made mention of any funds he might have had on hand as he bled to death in the sawdust near an overturned spitoon.

156

Chapter 19

It wasn't the first time it had happened. It went with the job. But as he and Billy Vail stared down at the body on the slab in the dim light of the Denver morgue, it sure beat all how little Grant Webber in death resembled the mental picture Longarm had formed of him.

The naked body of the dead killer seemed smaller than he'd imagined Webber as it lay there cold as a turkey from the ice chest with the Y-shaped incision of the autopsy roughly basted shut with butcher's twine. In embalmed repose, the blue-joweled face in fact hit the description, in that its black brows were bushy and the hair above the low forehead was straight and black enough for any Indian. Bill Schneider had said he'd known right off who he was talking to when the cuss had flashed a gold tooth in his face whilst claiming to be a cowhand named Shultz.

Longarm shook his head and said, "Funny. It almost seems as if I've seen that face before, and yet he still don't look as I've been seeing him in my imagination all this time."

Billy Vail was an old hand at such surprises. He said, "If you were suddenly to meet up with Julius Caesar and

Attila the Hun you'd be just as surprised by what they really looked like. Unless you've seen a photograph you're bound to picture them all wrong because when you hear a name you have to picture *some* face to go with it. What's eating you? Are you afraid Schneider shot the wrong cuss?"

Longarm said, "Not hardly. Not since those old boys who knew him up in Leadville came by to identify him. It's just . . . I dunno, I seem to be missing something here. No sign of that money in the rooming house he left the rest of his shit in?"

Vail said, "Forget it. It's gone. We've added it up with the help of the Lake County clerk and the Tabor Bank up yonder. Betwixt the price of that pig farm and other flashy spending along the way it adds up to that fifty grand, the five hundred he got for gunning the late Wig Gruber and some dirty money he'd likely made on the side as a lawman before they fired him."

Vail snorted cigar smoke out of his nostrils like a steamed but weary bull and added, "So we write him off as the last of the big-time spenders of Uncle Sam's dinero and Schneider done good. He saved the tax payers the expense of a trial!"

Longarm didn't argue. As they left the morgue he asked his boss what his next chore might be.

Vail said, "Want you to hang tight around the federal building for when Lake County sends for you. I sure wish real life was like one of them Ned Buntline Wild West novels where the hero gets to shoot ten *hombres malo*, kiss his pony, and ride the gal off into the sunset. But it ain't. So you have to show for that fool hearing, even though we all know they'll find *you* done good, too."

Out on the walk, Longarm glanced up at the sun, decided he'd only be asking for trouble if he asked for the rest of the afternoon off, and went back to the federal building with the old fart.

158

Once there he stayed out in the marble hallway as Vail entered the office, and when Vail didn't come back out to yell at him Longarm left by a side entrance for an early supper.

But when he went to escort Lilo from her hotel to the beer garden where she was working, they told him she'd checked out.

He asked if she'd left an address to forward any mail to. She had. It wasn't far and when he got there it turned out to be a rooming house. But when he asked they told him she'd already left for her evening job at the beer garden, with her beau.

Longarm said, "Oh, him?" and decided to quit whilst he was ahead. For a long-faced former lover staring through a whitewashed trellis at a gal whilst she waited tables could throw her off her stride and look sort of pathetical while he was at it.

Fortunately a certain young widow woman with light brown hair was receiving that evening at her Sherman Street brownstone and they'd both forgotten how swell they got along in the sack.

So she was sort of upset when he had to send word that Lake County had sent for him. He'd warned her they might. The hearing was set for a Wednesday afternoon. Longarm timed it to arrive a day early. He felt no call to tell anyone he was back in town before he'd hired a mount to ride out by Turquoise Lake in his denims with a pick and spade.

He stopped first at the Hendersens'. Walt Hendersen and Lars had driven all the stock from the now-abandoned pig farm over to their own holdings. Walt said the place was up for sale in the name of the late Edith Webber's kids, by order of the formidable Augusta Tabor. It was a hell of a way to get ahead in the world, but Walt Hendersen pointed out, and Longarm had to grudgingly agree,

159

the murdered gal's kids were likely to wind up richer than had she lived to raise the two of them.

Walt and Lars Hendersen followed Longarm back to the pig farm and watched with interest as he flooded the dirt floor of the cabin with pump water. He explained how he'd heard it was an old Hindu trick. He felt dumb when nothing happened as the dirt floor dried out even. They just looked at one another as he said, "Well, it was worth a try. Webber never took the money down to Denver with him."

Walt Hendersen said, "He'd have surely been stupid to leave it *here*, knowing he could never come back for it, wouldn't he?"

Longarm explained, "I was hoping he'd lit out whilst the lighting out was good. The kids would have noticed and asked what he was doing if he'd commenced to dig up the floor after murdering their mother."

Hendersen shrugged and asked, "What was to stop him from murdering two helpless kids?"

Longarm said, "I wish you hadn't said that, Walt. It's airtight. The bastard couldn't have left any buried treasure around here. Like my boss said, he must have spent it all."

They shook on that and parted friendly. Longarm had known better than to have hired the mount near the Taj Mahal and he'd checked into the old Tabor Hotel, this time. The Tabor Hotel was, in point of fact, rooms to let above the big general store Silver Dollar Tabor had started out from and still held on to for sentimental reasons or because he was a Scotsman and the layout still turned a profit.

Longarm found it made a swell hideout.

Next morning, after a good night's rest, alone, he dropped by the sheriff's department near the county courthouse to compare notes and they agreed to haul in some witnesses not named as such as yet by the county coroner.

160

After a light noon dinner consisting of eggs sunnyside up on a bed of chili con carne over the usual blue-plate special Longarm went over to the courthouse for the hearing.

Old Lyn Eddy was raising an awesome stink about being called in as a witness, swearing he'd never known the late Johnny Dart save in passing. Gus Steiner, the security chief at the Warmerbroder Mine, swore *he'd* never known Johnny Dart that well.

Longarm had only asked them to bring Roy Hawkins in, but the Powerful Patricia, Will Travis, and even little Cherry Poppins had shown up along with the part owner who'd actually witnessed the shooting at the bar that night.

The coroner seemed confused. He asked Longarm what all these other folk were doing there. Longarm said, "It'll all come out in the wash as I make my case, sir. Some of what I'm about to tell you and your panel may surprise you. I know it sure surprises me and I may need additional testimony to back my outrageous notions."

The county coroner, a sort of courtly gray-haired druggist when he wasn't holding inquests, told everybody in that case to be seated.

He and his panel of eight moved around to their own side of the long trellis table and sat down. The coroner banged his gavel and asked Longarm, seeing he was so smart, who they wanted to call first.

Longarm rose to reply, "I'd best go first."

So they swore him in and sat him down on the witness chair in front of them. He leaned back comfortably to begin, "I was never sent up here to even talk to the late Johnny Dart, alias Drake. I was sent to see if I could recover fifty thousand dollars, mostly in gold and taken at gunpoint from Camp Weld a few months back."

The corner said, "Read about the robbery. Two of the bandits were found floating down the South Platte. The

161

one who came up here holed up in a house of ill repute, was arrested in the same, and was hanged down in Denver. What's that got to do with you shooting Johnny Dart?"

Longarm said, "Nothing in a way, and something in another. The late Grant Webber, you may have read in the papers, more recent, had wound up so rich he had to explain himself by saying he'd won big at cards with the late Johnny Dart. All the money he *should* have had was the five-hundred-dollar bounty he got for gunning the former chief of security at the Warmerbroder Mine."

He turned to smile back at Gus Steiner as he added, "The one our Mr. Steiner is guarding now. His former boss, the late Wig Gruber, was wanted in other parts and Webber got no more than five hundred for what ammounted to cold-blooded murder."

He turned back to the panel to continue, "Wig Gruber had busted a few heads, mostly down-on-their-luck Cousin Jacks he caught trying to high-grade. So I naturally had to eliminate Cornish blood money before I could be certain Webber had come by his small fortune some other way."

The coroner said, "Hold on. You just told us Webber won the money at cards off Johnny Dart."

Longarm shook his head and said, "That's what Webber said. Once I learned their famous game never took place I knew the Cousin Jacks had never paid off Webber for killing Gruber for them in any way, shape, or form. Letting him win the money from one of their own would have been slick as a snake if, and *only* if, they'd had call to pay a dime to have Wig Gruber killed. But they never did. I have it on other good authority, who shall be nameless, Wig Gruber was working with Cornish high-graders who'd have never in this world wanted to see him dead."

He could almost hear old Eddy's sigh of relief behind him.

162

He continued, "I'd in point of fact lost interest in Johnny Dart as a witness by the time I was forced to shoot him. He'd played no part in the case I was on. He didn't know I'd dismissed him. He thought I wanted to talk to him about that killing out Nevada way. He drank too much to think straight by the time he thought I was catching up with him. There's no mystery about what happened then. Miss Cherry Poppins, present here this afternoon, warned me Dart was laying for me at the bar. He was. Roy Hawkins, also present, saw the simp go for his gun before I fired. I'm sure he'll so testify, but do you really care about such an open-and-shut case of self-defense? I'd have been within my rights to *back shoot* him. I'm a paid-up peace officer and he was a wanted murderer. Where outside a Ned Buntline romance does it say a lawman's required to challenge an armed-and-dangerous outlaw to an affair of honor?"

The coroner said, "By cracky, you're right. What are we holding this fool hearing for?"

Longarm mildly suggested, "Don't you want to hear who really paid the late Grant Webber to gun Wig Gruber in the Taj Mahal?"

"Do you know?" asked the coroner.

Longarm said, "Sure I do. Plain as the nose on one's guilty face as soon as you eliminate the Cousin Jacks and the Camp Weld payroll Grant Webber never found."

He flinched and rolled off his seat as a revolver barked thrice behind him. Longarm drew as he rolled to one side and came back up with his six-gun peering into all that gun smoke in the back of the hearing room.

To his relief a familiar voice called out, "I got him, Longarm! He stood up and threw down on you from behind, just like you said he might!"

The coroner got to his feet, peering into the swirling gun smoke to demand, "Who are you jawing about, Deputy Quinn? What's going on here this afternoon?"

163

Longarm holstered his .44-40 as he moved back to join his Lake County pard over the sprawled body at his feet. Calling back to the coroner and other confounded witnesses, Longarm said, "Gus Steiner just now broke cover, as we hoped he might, when he saw I was getting warm. He aimed to kill me before I could tell you he paid his fellow Dutchman and mayhaps a kinsman to kill his boss, Wig Gruber."

Staring soberly down at the dead two-face, he added, "The hell of it was, I didn't have a *federal charge* on him that would have stuck if he'd just hung tough. Wig Gruber was wanted by the law and as I just now said, it ain't nice but it ain't murder when a lawman guns a wanted killer dirty. Webber would have hanged for murdering his woman. This murdersome rascal was just done in by his own guilty conscience. Had he just sat tight I'd have run out of steam and he'd still be the security chief drawing more from his high-grading pals than his absentee employers!"

A member of the panel piped up, "But what was his *motive* for having his own boss gunned by . . . a cousin you say?"

The coroner snapped, "Shut up and set down, Carson! Ain't you been paying attention at all?"

Longarm said, "I was struck by the possible family resemblance as I viewed the late Grant Webber shortly after he became late. I could be wrong, of course. The two of them could have simply cut a deal to get Gruber out of the way so's Steiner, here, could take over the good thing he had going for himself. In any event, Steiner paid handsomely to have Gruber shot. He could afford to. He was making money hand over fist by the time Gruber was cold in his grave."

As all he'd said sank in, everyone there moved closer to view the remains and tell Longarm how smart he was. The Powerful Patricia put her arm through his and purred, "We knew you could do it, Custis! But I'm missing something, here. If Webber never found that government payroll . . ."

Longarm said, "You ain't missing nothing, Miss Patricia. Me and the tax payers of these United States are the ones missing something. That payroll money was never recovered by anybody. It's all still out there, waiting to be found, if I had any notion where to start!"

Chapter 20

Gunshots in the afternoon attracted attention, even in the middle of Leadville. Among those drawn to the sounds of Deputy Quinn's six-gun were Freedom Ford and two other reporters from the nearby office of the *Herald Democrat*. Longarm could only hope the nearby Powerful Patricia would take it as professional concern when Freedom flung herself against Longarm in the crowd assembled to gasp, "Custis, what have you been up to *now*, you naughty thing! You never came by to let me know you were back in town, and what's all this we just heard about a coroner's hearing and yet another shoot-out?"

The coroner saved the situation by banging for order and telling one and all to, dammit, be seated whilst he sorted things out.

Longarm sat Freedom and her shorthand notes to one side to whisper a terse outline of what she'd missed, so far.

Meanwhile the coroner and his panel decided by voice vote that since they the jury had just witnessed the shooting of Gus Steiner they had no call to convene any future hearings on *that* dumb son of a bitch. It was decided his death had been suicide by three bullets in the back at

166

point-blank range, the probable motive being despondency at the prospect of losing his job once the queers he worked for found out he'd been out to rob them worse than the late Wig Gruber had.

Once the combined final verdict was read off, the coroner declared the hearing ended. So the Powerful Patricia came over to hook an arm through Longarm's. He perforce introduced her to Freedom Ford of the *Herald Democrat*. The Powerful Patricia said she preferred to read the *Rocky Mountain News*, and the reporter sweetly purred, "Oh, you can *read*, my dear?"

Cherry Poppins had heard the last of their exchange as she came to join them, falling in on Longarm's other side to chortle, "I can read. Sort of. I've been taking lessons since I've become a fucking lady."

The bemused newspaper gal said, "Well good on you, Miss . . . ?"

Longarm introduced them, having no call to explain to either how he might have met the other.

Deputy Quinn and another county lawman saved the day, for the moment, by coming over to ask who was stuck with the cadaver of the late Gus Steiner. They held it hardly seemed fair he should be buried at Lake County's expense when he'd been out to murder a federal man.

Longarm gently but firmly replied, "Only in the vain hopes of covering up his semilegitimate killing of Wig Gruber and the pure-illegal grand larceny out to the Warmerbroder Mine. I suspect, when push comes to shove, Lake County and the Bureau of Mines, betwixt them, ought to be able to get the twisted sisters to bury him, stuff him, whatever, seeing they *hired* both crooks."

The county men said that sounded fair and left to report what had just happened to their own superiors. Will Travis came over to gather up Cherry Poppins and the Powerful Patricia, if they aimed to ride on back to the Carbonate Spa in *his* buggy.

As they trailed after Travis, the Powerful Patricia archly trilled over her shoulder they'd be expecting him for the supper show.

Freedom Ford sniffed. "I'll bet they both do their hair with the same bottle of stove blacking! The one who calls herself a 'fucking lady' seems to like you best. So, what's the story?"

Aware of the other reporters' pretending to talk to others, Longarm said, "You have my words as an enlisted man and gentleman I have never fucked that lady. As for the story, it ain't over yet and I'll be proud to give you another . . . exclusive, before I leave town."

The innocent-looking brown-haired gal blinked and whispered, "You *suspect* those dance hall girls of something, Custis?"

He said, "They don't work in a dance hall. But everyone's a suspect until proven innocent."

That seemed to satisfy her. He'd noticed she was easier than some to satisfy, Lord love her.

So Freedom Ford went after the coroner to pester him for things to put in her paper and Longarm discreetly slipped out a side door before anybody could ask where he was going.

Where he went was the big brick Tabor Bank, near his Silver Dollar Saloon. Longarm went in and asked to speak to the branch manager. After some whispering off to one side about his store-bought suit versus his federal badge, a big shot sat him down and offered him a cigar. But when Longarm told them what he wanted, the branch manager told him, "I fear such information is privileged, sir. We are not authorized to give out information about our customers' deposits or withdrawals."

Longarm put the fancy cigar away to save for somebody ugly as he pointed out, "I could always ankle over to the courthouse for a court order."

The banker sniffed. "Not in Lake County you couldn't.

This bank is the personal property of Horace 'Silver Dollar' Tabor, our current mayor and de facto boss of the Lake County political machine."

The banker let that sink in and added, "*He* could tell us to let you poke through our files. There's not a judge in this county who would dare to!"

Longarm said, "We'll see. I take it old Hod and his Baby Doe are still in residence at the Claredon House?"

The banker stiffly declared that was none of his concern. Longarm thanked him for nothing much and grumped his way out just as another snot shut the front door behind him and hung up a sign marked CLOSED.

Longarm considered letting it go. Billy Vail had written off the missing money and they'd only sent him back up this way for the hearing just now ended. So what the hell.

So he trudged on down to the fancy Claredon House—you called a hotel a *house* when it was really fancy—and the snooty room clerk managed not to laugh at Longarm as he informed him in a lofty tone that "the Tabors," as they were already commencing to call the old goat and his beautiful but dumb mistress, had departed for Denver on business.

Longarm thanked him anyhow and turned away. They had a swamping pier glass near the entrance, put there so's ladies of fashion about to leave for church or the opera could make sure nothing needed to be shored up. Longarm's reflected image looked all right to Longarm, but seeing he had the time he found a tailor shop near Front and State where they could steam and press tweed whilst you waited.

After that he treated himself to a set-down shave, he didn't need a haircut, and had them splash him with bay rum. By the time he felt less laughable it was going on supper time. He found a chili joint and washed down his light repast of tamales, enchiladas, and chili verde with plenty of black coffee before he ankled on up past the Taj Mahal to the Carbonate Spa.

The cavernous wine theater was dimly lit, and as he passed through on his way to the bar he spied little Cherry Poppins seated alone at one table, sipping wine or whatever through a straw.

He moved over to sit down across from her, confessing, "I reckon I won't be here come morning. But seeing I'm here for the night I might as well take in this evening's show and . . . Miss Patricia anywhere on the premises, Miss Cherry?"

She said, "Having supper with Mister Travis and his wife at their house. Roy Hawkins is with her. Are you still mad at Roy Hawkins? He thinks you are."

Longarm shrugged and said, "Life's too short to be at feud with its petty annoyances. He backed my story at the hearing this afternoon. So what the hey. What's that you're drinking, it don't look like wine."

She said, "It ain't. It's ginger beer. It's sweeter than wine and I like it better. You want me to fetch you some?"

He said, "Not just yet, thanks. Just had supper. Ain't ready to drink nothing stronger than coffee this early. You serve much of that Hindu joy juice here at the Carbonate Spa, Miss Cherry?"

She nodded and said, "The ladies who come in like it better. That's how come I prefers it, now that, thanks to you and Miss Patricia, I have become a fucking lady."

She reached across the table to put her hand on his wrist as she added in a choked tone, "I never knew I could be a fucking lady before you treated me like one, Custis! Most of the men I've ever known have treated me . . . like I was *nobody*. You make me feel like I might be . . . *somebody*. I wish there was some way I could show you how I feel about that. But you don't want to fuck me, do you?"

He asked if she knew where they got their ginger beer,

explaining they made their own at the only other place in town he knew that served it.

Cherry Poppins said, "The barkeep tells me they buy it off some lady named Miss Binnie, here in town. She brews it in jars from some plant that comes from India and . . . Where are you going, Custis?"

He didn't answer. He tore out the front and along the walk down to the Taj Mahal at a pace that turned heads in the gloaming light.

At the Taj Mahal he told the harem gal named Joy he had to see her boss lady right away. Joy led him up those same stairs, told him to hold his horses, and went down the corridor to vanish for a million years before a familiar voice called out, "Custis, where are you? Come here! I need you!"

Joy shut the door after him with a smirk as Longarm rejoined the voluptuous Binnie Bodmin on her mushroom of silk pillows. She wasn't smoking her bubble pipe, or wearing any clothes, as she asked him why he was still dressed and in that ridiculous upright position.

Longarm said, "I'm on duty. Before I take my pants off, further along when I know more about it, what's this I hear about you selling ginger beer to the Carbonate Spa, Miss Binnie?"

She propped herself up on one elbow, naked as a jay, to favor him with a puzzled smile as she replied, "What of it, Custis? You'd seen my shelves and shelves of ginger beer. Did you think I drank all of it myself? The people who own that other wine theater are Cornish as well, and they're too far up the street for serious rivalry. So one hand washes the other and Will Travis gets me a good price on imported Mexican tequila. Why are we having this dumb conversation, dear? I have nothing to hide from you. Look!"

He had to laugh as she rolled on her back to spread her thighs. He said, "I might take you up on that, later tonight.

171

Right now I'd like you to listen tight. You told me that other time Abner Prentiss did spend one night here at the Taj Mahal. I fear I was distracted when you said you'd sent him on up State Street to another establishment. I took it for granted you meant that house of ill repute where they arrested him."

She sat up again to pout, "Custis Long, do I look like the sort of woman who'd know anyone running a whore-house?"

He thought it undiplomatic to answer that honestly. He smiled at her sheepishly and replied, "I just said you had me distracticated. So let's ask the question again. Did you steer that troubled youth on up to Madame Three Tits's, or just as far as your Cornish cousins at the Carbonate Spa?"

The white-haired temptress marveled, "Does anyone really have three tits? Of course I suggested he try the Carbonate Spa. They don't have as many rooms for hire upstairs. But they have some. As to whether he stayed there or panted his way on up to that freak show, I just don't know, Custis. I never laid eyes on the wayward youth again. I never *heard* of him again until I heard he'd been arrested and hauled away. Why would I lie? What does it matter?"

Longarm said he believed her. As he rolled off the pile of pillows she rose like a naked Venus from the waves to follow him to her doorway and grind her white pubic thatch against his tobacco-brown tweed as they parted friendly.

It was getting darker as he moved back up State Street at a more thoughtful pace, gathering his thoughts as he tried to sort the sheep from the goats and deciding Cherry Poppins was likely innocent for certain.

Back at the Carbonate Spa, the musicians were in the orchestra pit tuning their instruments. The footlight hadn't been lit yet. The overhead lamps had been trimmed, so

172

the cavernous wine theater was poorly lit and hazy with tobacco smoke as Cherry Poppins and another waitress served the couples at scattered tables, with half of them still vacant.

Longarm found the Powerful Patricia talking to Roy Hawkins by their bar. The statuesque brunette still wore the dress she'd worn to supper at their partner's place. When she saw him the Powerful Patricia smiled and said, "Custis! Cherry told us you were by earlier! We just got back and I was so afraid you'd . . . find something else to do."

He said, "I did. How come you never told me Abner Prentiss spent a night or more upstairs, above this very wine theater?"

She blinked and said, "I didn't know he had!" She turned to Hawkins to demand, "Might you know anything about this, Roy?"

Hawkins stared down at the floor, shrugged, and confessed in a hangdog tone, "It didn't seem important. I let him use that guest room when he approached me late one rainy night, offering a week's salary if we'd take him in. I let him flop upstairs, just that one time, and suggested that parlor house up the way was more his style. I swear I didn't know he was wanted until after they'd arrested him. Once they had, I felt no call to bother you or Will about it."

The Powerful Patricia called him a stupid ass and asked Longarm where they were going from there.

He said, "Upstairs. I want to look at the room he described as 'above a wine theater!' "

The Powerful Patricia said that made two of them and took the lead. Longarm followed her up the stairs with Roy Hawkins bringing up the rear. As they rose through the smoke-filled gloom the big brunette in the lead warned, "Watch your step, Custis."

173

Before he could assure her he was, the gloom was rent by the shrill voice of Cherry Poppins, screaming, "Oh! No! Custis! Behind you!"

And then all hell broke loose.

Chapter 21

As Longarm spun on the dark stairs, slapping leather, one heel came down in the middle of the air. So he fell on his rump as the two-faced Roy Hawkins put a derringer round between Longarm's shoulder blades, had he still been following the two-faced Powerful Patricia.

Since he wasn't, he fired from his seated position on the stairs to put two hundred grains of hot lead in the would be back-shooter's chest. Falling ass over tea kettle down all those uncarpeted stair risers didn't do him a whole lot of good, either.

Then Longarm almost followed Hawkins head first as the considerable limp weight of the Powerful Patricia came down the same stairs from above to bounce off Longarm's back and keep going while he clung for dear life to a banister upright. By now the floor below was nigh empty as patrons dashed outside in panic, some never to return lest they have to pay for all that wine they were leaving behind.

Others, made of sterner stuff, stayed put or even moved closer as Longarm rose to follow the smoking muzzle of his six-gun down to join the pileup at the foot of the stairs.

It was Cherry Poppins who gently rolled the Powerful

Patricia off Roy Hawkins and took the dying woman's head in her lap as she sat on her own knees. Cherry Poppins pleaded, "Please don't die on me, Miss Patricia!"

One of the entertainers from backstage joined Longarm to stand over the Powerful Patricia in his clown's outfit, holding a slapstick.

Longarm hunkered down betwixt the gals and the face-up cadaver of Roy Hawkins. You could tell he was a cadaver as soon as you felt the side of his neck in vain for a pulse.

The Powerful Patricia opened her eyes to stare up through Longarm at the gun smoke drifting closer to the ceiling as she sighed, "I told you to let me handle it. I told you I had him wrapped around my finger and . . . Why are you wearing that silly outfit, Roy?"

The clown explained he was with the show. She never heard him. Longarm reached out with his free hand to close her eyelids. Cherry Poppins began to cry.

Considering all those police whistles trilling out on State Street, it took a spell for Mart Duggan in the flesh and a corporal's squad of lesser lawmen to bull their way in. Duggan took in the scene thoughtfully before he remarked, "Looks like the last scene of *Hamlet*. Who shot whom and how come?"

Longarm got back to his feet and commenced to reload as he replied in a still-uncertain tone, "I was following Miss Patricia up them stairs. He was behind me. The temptation must have been too much for him. He fired at my spine with that derringer over against yon baseboard. Thanks to the way Miss Cherry, there, let me know in time, Hawkins missed me and nailed his business partner and likely secret lover in the aorta, judging by the way she died just now. As to how come, I'm still working on that. I'd like to go topside and look, if that's all right with you."

The flamboyant-but-fair town tamer told one of the

176

Leadville lawmen with him to take charge of the death scene and asked Longarm what they were waiting for.

Longarm put his six-gun away and led off. They didn't find shit in any of those other rooms Roy Hawkins had lied about in hopes of throwing off the quick-witted Longarm.

In the front room above the wine theater, a room that now held bitter-sweet memories of perfumed hair and soft tits in the lamplight for Longarm, he got a good grip on the posts of the bed he'd never forget and swung it around to almost block the door. Marshal Duggan hunkered down beside him as Longarm held the lamp closer to the pin planking the bed had been shading. It was Duggan who said, "Those nail heads are one size larger, here in the middle, than anywhere else!"

Longarm set the lamp on the planks to one side as he got out his pocketknife, observing, "When you replace a nail you've pulled out of softwood you want to replace it with a bigger one to grip the sides of the nail hole."

As he got to work with a blade usually used to turn screws, Duggan asked if a crowbar wouldn't be faster.

Longarm nodded but said, "I can have a plank loose in the time it would take you to fetch one. Only need to pry up one when the flooring is pine."

He proved his point, once he had one end of one plank to where he could hook the fingers of his other hand around the sawed pine. Duggan laughed and said, "Remind me never to arm wreste you for serious money!" whilst Longarm pulled and nails squealed like piglets.

After that it only took moments to manhandle the other renailed planks out of the way. Abner Prentiss had only pried up four short lengths for his own devices.

There wasn't all that much to see for Longarm's effort. He reached for the lamp, though it didn't help much. The pressed-tin ceiling of the wine theater below had been nailed directly to the bottoms of the joists. The embossed metal facing up was galvanized sheet iron instead of actual tin plate. It was still fairly shiny, thanks to the thin dry air and protection from the smelter fumes betwixt the joists. After that it just hung there. Anything anyone had ever hidden under the flooring of the Powerful Patricia's bedroom seemed long gone.

Then as Longarm wig-wagged the oil lamp he spied something almost out of reach, set the lamp down, and lay flat to reach for and recover a twenty-dollar double eagle.

Holding it up to Duggan's view Longarm said, "This must be the place. It wasn't always Miss Patricia's bedroom. They were hiring it out, no questions asked, when the bank robbing Abner Prentiss spent a night here. With both of them dead the details are moot. It's clear they figured him for trouble, fixed him up with Madame Three Tits for a while, and then they turned him in to *you*, once they found the loot he'd hidden *here*! Miss Cherry told me how the poor simp liked to order wine downstairs, gloating at the ceiling now and again. We'll never know for certain, but he may have come back up here now and again to make withdrawels. If he did, that would be how Miss Patricia and Roy Hawkins caught on to where and what he had hidden here."

Duggan nodded soberly and said, "He may have told them, seeing all of them were as crooked. But they had to get rid of a right dangerous crook indeed before they dared to help themselves to his money!"

Longarm pocketed the gold coin as evidence and got to his feet, dusting his tweed with his Stetson as he pointed out, "It wasn't his money. Every dime of it was the property of these United States and I, dammit, *showered* up here with the aid of the modern plumbing that Jezebel had installed with part of the loot!"

"When was that, Longarm?" Duggan asked.

Longarm said, "Long ago when I was young and still

178

thought the world might be run on the level. Let's go down and make sure Will Travis and his family don't leave town before I can have a serious talk with him and the bank examiners in the cold gray dawn!"

Duggan allowed it might be nice if Longarm were to sign another deposition regarding those bodies at the foot of the stairs. So Billy Vail was fit to be tied in Denver, but Longarm was stuck in Leadville over the weekend, busy as a one-armed paper hanger in a wind storm.

A teary-eyed Cherry Poppins showed up at his hotel door in the wee small hours asking if they could shack up or, failing that, whether he wanted her to go back to being a whore instead of a fucking lady.

Longarm told her to wait in the hall, shut the door long enough to fish out five dollars, and told her to check into another hotel closer to the narrow gauge depot and sit tight 'til he picked her up there on his way back to Denver.

As she scampered off like a kid leaving school for the day Longarm went back to bed with Freedom Ford.

As she continued their interview in depth, dog style, the brown-haired famous journalist asked what on earth he meant to do in Denver with the most notorious whore of Leadville. Gripping a shapely bare hip in each palm as he continued their interview, Longarm confessed, "I have no idea. But she saved my life, twice, and she don't want to be a whore no more."

Freedom arched her spine to take it deeper as she lowered her cheek to the pillow to purr, "This does feel nicer when you do it with somebody you like. You were telling me how they had you so flimflammed at first, dear?"

Longarm said, "I was. I wish they wouldn't do that. Your average crook has less than average brains. That's how come he or she decides to be a crook. Honesty ain't the best policy because the angels are watching your every move. *Dis*honesty is just too blamed expensive for what

179

you might get out of it versus what you might have to lose. If the story we got from Will Travis this evening holds up when we examine the books, he'll still own a wine theater on State Street making money hand over fist. It would have been in his crooked partner's own best interests just to go on making money the safe way. But they got greedy and acted like a pair of dumb kids."

She murmured, "A little more to the left and . . . Oooh, nice! Why did it take you so long to catch on if they were simply greedy kids, dear?"

He said, "I was confounded by *other* greedy kids working at cross-purpose to make me suspect I was playing chess when the name of the game was only checkers. That happens to you once you build a rep as a lawman of some ability. Crooks I was never sent after kept thinking I'd been sent after them with results that were mighty confusing before I had all the puzzle pieces in separate piles. Grant Webber had taken part in the arrest of Abner Prentiss, but he'd never known anything about the money taken from Camp Weld. He'd been paid off, earlier, to kill that Wig Gruber I told you about. Then he'd lied about winning it at cards with yet another killer, with his own guilty conscience, before he murdered his woman all by his fool self. So, like I said, I wasted a whole lot of effort and came close to getting my fool self killed asking questions about things they never sent me up this way to find out!"

She said, "I'm glad. Can we turn me over and finish more . . . romantic?"

They could. They did. He was afraid they'd hear her out on the street as she gave vent to her romantic feelings.

He enjoyed them, too. There was a lot to be said for little brown-haired girls as strong or stronger than statuesque brunettes.

The interview continued, at less depth, as they cuddled against the pillows backed up by the headboard to share

a smoke she considered a tad depraved. Freedom Ford
had the makings of a great journalist, as well as a great
lay. So Longarm found himself sidestepping questions
about other headboards they might have held pillow conversations against or other conversations entire atop other
pillows with others who had their own rights to privacy.

She never asked him how he'd known so much about
the Powerful Patricia's bedroom. It sure beat all how
women tended just to miss like that. She kept nagging
and nagging him about that waif he'd just sent off into
the night and he was commencing to find it tedious to
assure her he had never even considered getting romantic
with Cherry Poppins.

He said, "I owe her. Like I told you, I recruited her
from a house of ill repute to help me with my mission
and she came through for me with flying colors. She was
watching my back, more than once, when I should have
been less trusting. She got that waitress job at the Carbonate Spa on her own. Will Travis says he's fixing to
put the place up for sale. Miss Cherry's too notorious in
Leadville to stay here in any case. I'm hoping to find her
another position down in Denver."

"Really? With Emma Gould or Madame Ruth Jacobs?"
the too-sharp-by-half newspaper gal asked with a Mona
Lisa smile.

So Longarm never told her what he had in mind and it
served her right for being such a wiseass, as great as her
ass might be.

After that one night of love, a serious morning with the
bank examiners after Billy Vail had gotten Silver Dollar
Tabor out of bed at the flashy Windsor House in Denver
to send some sizzling telegrams, and yet another pesky
coroners inquest, sent that afternoon by sizzling wires
from Governor Fred Pitkin, Longarm was free to go.

The joint estates of the late business partners of the
fortunate Will Travis came to over fifty grand and let him

off the hook. He still said he might sell out and take up something easier on the nerves, like say prospecting in Apache country.

So the following Monday evening, down in Denver, Cherry Poppins sat cooling her heels, alone, in the front parlor of an imposing brownstone pile on the corner of Sherman and 12th Avenue on Capitol Hill. The straw boater Longarm had bought her to go with her new calico pinafore itched a scalp that she'd been abusing. She'd taken it off to hold in her lap like a basket of flowers whilst her escort and their hostess, the great and wonderful Augusta Tabor, decided her fate in the sewing room.

The no-longer-young helpmate Silver Dollar Tabor had set aside with a whole lot of money in favor of a divorcée with neither the brains nor the new morals of Cherry Poppins had never been a great beauty. But in her day she'd listened to his windy brags, backed his wild dreams, and bore him a son as she'd followed her lumbering man and his bushy mustache up the Republican fork of the Kansas River to Pikes Peak and busted.

Starting over on money *she* made, taking in washing, the already-middle aged Hod Tabor begged, borrowed, or built his general store in Slabtown and let his faithful Augusta run it whilst he chased butterfly mining ventures. So they commenced to get rich, stuck in one place a spell, as she weighed out bacon and flower, sold dynamite or mining tools, and ran a post office in the back, where she'd been the one sorting mail.

But all that was ancient history, as was the time Longarm and his pal Sergeant Nolan of the Denver P.D. had saved the very house they sat in from being ransacked by those burglars.

Longarm had never called in that favor both Tabors had declared they owed him, until that evening. The plain-featured-but-somehow-regal Augusta Tabor listened quietly as he brought her up to date on more recent events

182

and explained his debt to the social outcast awaiting any fate the now-very-social Augusta Tabor might come up with.

When she told Longarm to bring Cherry Poppins in he warned her soberly, "We've cleaned her up a heap and an army doc I asked to look her over says she ain't got nothing that's catching. But she ain't exactly . . . couth, Miss Augusta."

The older woman sighed and said, "I was a working girl in Leadville when it was still Slabtown and don't think I was never tempted. Bring her in and let's have a look at her, Custis."

Longarm did, warning Cherry Poppins along the way to mind herself. So as they entered the sewing room Cherry Poppins attempted to curtsy, dropped her hat, and said, "Shit!"

The imposing Augusta laughed as Longarm bent red-faced to pick up the hat. She asked the young whore if she was aware the roots of her black hair seemed to be coming out blond.

Cherry Poppins replied, "Yes, ma'am, I dyed my hair black so's the men who fucked me when I was a whore wouldn't recognize me where I was waiting tables. I don't want to be a whore no more. I want to be a fucking lady, like you!"

Augusta Tabor suddenly seemed twenty years younger when she laughed like a mean little kid and told Longarm, "I'll take over from here. So why don't you run along and let us share some girl talk?"

Longarm knew things were going to be all right when the last thing he heard, as he was leaving, was the regal Denver dowager telling Cherry Poppins, "Before we decide anything else, my dear, we're going to have to do something about that fucking hair!"

Watch for

LONGARM AND THE BANK ROBBER'S DAUGHTER

301st novel in the exciting LONGARM series from Jove

Coming in December!

LONGARM

Explore the exciting Old West with one of the men who made it wild!

JAKE LOGAN
TODAY'S HOTTEST ACTION WESTERN!